THE KIVA AND THE MOSQUE

THE KIVA AND THE MOSQUE

KAYT C. PECK

SAPPHIRE BOOKS

SALINAS, CALIFORNIA

This and other Sapphire Books titles can be found at
www.sapphirebooks.com

Dedication

To an ancient people called the Anastasi who have long inspired my imagination. To Yanar Mohammad and the women of the Organization of Women's Freedom in Iraq (OWFI). It was an honor to have worked with you and learned from you. In some small way, I hope this book can improve the world in which we all live.

Acknowledgment

To Sapphire Books for giving my work a public voice and for their whole team of "sisters" who believe in the power of the written word.

Chapter One

The Kiva

A tourist dressed in wrinkled khaki shorts and an equally wrinkled T-shirt used the camera on his cell phone to snap a picture of an ancient cliff dwelling. Kidwell Brown stood patiently behind him. His bulk occupied most of the width of the paved trail, giving her little choice but to wait for the path to clear.

"Mort will shit a brick when he sees this," the tourist said. He switched from using the instrument as a camera to a telephone. "He loves all this Indian stuff." His teenage son stood waiting near the entrance of a structure that had once been a home for a culture that no longer existed.

"Yeah, Dad," the youth said, not trying to hide the boredom in his voice, "can we stop at the casino on our way back to Santa Fe?"

The man ignored his son as he held the phone to his ear. After a pause, he lowered the device and looked at the display.

"God damn it," he said. "How can people stand to live here? There isn't even cell signal."

The man returned the phone to the case on his belt and lumbered along the trail, finally opening the path. He huffed and pulled himself up using the handrails when the trail became in the least bit steep. Kidwell suspected that the man spent his days in an office building, his only exercise being a regular walk to the break room. A woman whom Kidwell assumed was the man's wife leaned out a doorway just a short climb above them. A replica of the ladders originally used by the structure's inhabitants allowed visitors to climb into that part of the dwelling. As the man detoured toward his wife's call, the mildly sadistic urge to watch him struggle up the ladder tempted Kidwell. Instead, she smiled to herself and continued down the path.

When she was younger, Kidwell would have been angry and offended at the man's lack of awareness of not only the people around him, but of the sacredness of the place where he now walked. Years and experience gradually cured her of most of her once strong need to convince others how they should see the world. Life was too short and too precious to waste her energy on such a futile effort.

Besides, she had no time for such foolishness this day. A magnetic urge drew her to one of her strongest sacred places. The intensity of that urge lessened any distraction caused by a passing tourist. Kidwell had first discovered Bandelier National Monument and the Anastasi in her youth. It felt like home the first time she climbed a rough ladder into the interior of an Anastasi dwelling. Twenty years passed before she dared tell anyone of the voices she heard while inside that room. The echo of voices and laughter from the valley below brought tears to her young eyes. Despite the fact that the language was none she knew, she felt warmth, love, and a sense of belonging at the sound. Only Anna, the soulmate she had once despaired of ever finding, knew that story or that a similar experience happened to Kidwell with almost every visit to an Anastasi site.

Kidwell had not needed to explain the details, for Anna shared the experience, and had since her own youth. Such memories drew them both to the Land of Enchantment and finally to meeting each other. Anna felt free to share her story over the decades, but Kidwell remained silent. During two decades in the Navy, such tales would likely have landed her a psychiatric review.

Today, Anna was not at her side. Kidwell awoke that morning, knowing she must walk the path to the Ceremonial Cave at Bandelier. As Kidwell told her sleepily languid lover of the need, Anna had been equally certain that her fate was for a quiet day in the backwoods home they shared. That had not been a problem. Independence was much of what assured the two women's togetherness.

Kidwell had nearly bypassed the paved path to the dwellings nearest the tourist center, but she could not resist the urge to weave through the tourists and seek an empty room, a place to listen quietly for a few moments. She found her moment about one hundred feet farther along the path. She climbed into an unoccupied room, moving toward the cool and inviting shadows at the back. It felt like slipping into the earth's womb when she entered such a place. She sat cross-legged on the floor and sought stillness. A whisper came, not the voices from the valley below as she usually experienced. It was nearby and mildly urgent. The words were foreign but she knew the meaning.

"Go on," it whispered, "she waits."

Kidwell's heart rate increased. Her experiences before only involved a feeling of familiarity in the voices she heard. Never before had she had such clarity in the meaning.

So the Ceremonial Cave it was. Kidwell eased herself down the ladder and onto the path. She increased her pace and took the shortest route possible from the paved path and onto the trail used by day hikers and backpackers more than passing tourists. The Ceremonial Cave trail did not draw the large numbers of tourists seeking sites high on experience and low on effort.

What is this all about? she wondered. She did not doubt her sanity, although she had in her younger days, before she accepted her "gift."

Although she kept her sense of purpose, Kidwell enjoyed the hike on the trail beside the river. It was a nice hike before she reached the fork where she'd turn to the northeast, taking the path to the ladders that were the precarious last effort in reaching the Ceremonial Cave. As she walked, she enjoyed the lush green smell of the willows, horsetails, and a smattering of pine trees in the growth that followed the stream, a trickle of water bringing life to the desert lands. There was little similarity to the ecosystem of the streambed and the rising canyon walls just a hundred feet higher. There was even less of a resemblance to the desert land stretching above the canyon rim. When she heard the movement of a large animal in the brush beside the trail, Kidwell wasn't surprised. She stopped, looking intently toward the sound, striving to identify the creature. Probably deer, she thought, but she remained watchful. She didn't have the panicky fear of bears that plagued most people, but she did have total and utter respect for the usually gentle giants. She and Anna had achieved a peaceful coexistence with the bears living in the forest surrounding their home. They were careful not to leave dog food out overnight, and they hung birdfeeders in trees several yards from the house and high enough so that a bear could not reach them. Leaving such calling cards was a hazard to humans and an injustice to bears. Such carelessness offered an invitation for a bear to live off human food and, in time, a likely signing of a death warrant for the animal. When a bear threatened a human, Fish and Game would do what they must.

While Kidwell and Anna sought to discourage bears around their home, they regularly encountered the magnificent animals while hiking or cutting firewood in the surrounding forests. They met one large female so often that they'd named her Gerty, enjoying sightings of the bear and her current cub or cubs which Gerty nurtured until they were ready to go out on their own. Gerty knew Kidwell and Anna, and they knew Gerty. Hence Gerty did not threaten them when they rounded a bend and surprised the bear and her two cubs as they scratched through a deadfall log, eating paws-full of assorted insects and grubs. In surprise, she'd risen on her back haunches, preparing to threaten, but then Gerty recognized her intruders. She dropped back to all fours, and then nuzzled her two cubs to the forefront. She sat and looked at the two women, as though to say, "See my children. Aren't they beautiful?" Although Kidwell and Anna kept a tight grip on their walking sticks, they each spent a few moments complementing Gerty's beautiful cubs. Then Gerty rounded up her young and herded them down a path running along Cabo Lucero Creek. Now and again, Kidwell and Anna retold the story to each other—and to anyone else who would listen—just because the event was such a pleasure to relive.

Today would be a much less hazardous

encounter. Kidwell watched two white tail does as they grazed their way through the brush beside the stream. Kidwell smiled a soft smile of deep pleasure and then continued her walk to the cave.

When Kidwell reached the base of the first of two ladders, she took a deep breath and readied herself for the climb. While in the Navy and not long after she'd retired, Kidwell had barely noticed the exertion of climbing the hundred feet to the cave above. She laughed quietly at herself as she mentally promised herself to return to "fighting fitness." She laughed because she knew she wouldn't, but that she would be forever compelled to have the same thought every time she faced this ladder.

Exertion or not, the climb was well worth it. When Kidwell stepped off the last rung and into the cave (not more than a large alcove actually) that protected and housed the kiva, she paused, partially to catch her breath but mainly to enjoy the view of the valley below and to feel the holiness of the place. As she looked down to the trail below, she saw a young man hiking her direction. She estimated he was only twenty minutes from the kiva. A feeling of disappointment and urgency caused her to turn from the view and walk rapidly to the kiva entrance. Kidwell looked down into the opening in the earth and grasped the top of the ladder.

When she reached the third rung, her life forever changed.

Blindly, Kidwell finished the last few steps to the floor of the kiva. Kidwell saw light but not much else. As her eyes adjusted to the brightness, objects clarified in her vision. She was not at the foot of the ladder, but hovering a few feet from the floor. She looked at the body lying near the ladder. She felt no surprises or shock even as she realized her own body lay beneath her.

Am I dead? she thought, amazingly undisturbed.

"Welcome," someone said.

Actually, "said" is not entirely correct. The word was clear but Kidwell had a sense that neither a voice nor her ears were involved in the process. As she turned to face the voice, Kidwell sensed floating, a movement powered entirely by will and intent instead of mind and muscle.

She saw a figure hovering, as she was, just a few feet off the floor. The figure was the source of the light, and, in the brightness, Kidwell could make out the shape of a woman.

"I'm honored," Kidwell answered, surprised at her own sense of calm.

"Do you know who I am?" the spirit asked.

Kidwell did, but she was at a loss as to how she knew. There was an impression of long, dark hair, and the fringe of a doeskin dress, but those clues would not have been enough alone.

"White Buffalo Calf Woman," Kidwell answered.

"That is the name some give me," the spirit answered, the voice deepening as it spoke. As the voice deepened, the shape changed, becoming male, bearded, and wearing a coarse one-piece garment. "I have others."

"Jesus," Kidwell said. Somewhere inside her, a place where she was still capable of simple human emotion, she felt a deep reverence and awe.

"Does the name matter?" the spirit asked.

"No, it doesn't," Kidwell answered, knowing that whatever form the spirit took, she would know it for what it was. In that instant, she knew she had been in its presence many times, during a sunset or while cruising in the middle of the ocean; the time she'd witnessed the birth of a child when she and the senior-chief she was with had stopped to aid a Saudi woman by the side of the road. She knew this feeling. She knew this awe.

"Why did you call me?" Kidwell asked.

"You are needed."

"Me? I can't do anything. Why me?"

"Because you listened."

"What do you need of me?"

"Tell all that Desert Lighting has no power."

"What?"

"You must go to the land of the Lone Wolf to meet your ally."

"I don't understand."

"When you seek truth with an open heart and an open mind, you will find it. Trust what you find there."

"I…I don't think I'm worthy. I don't understand."

"Answers will come as you need them. The time has come for a healing, or an ending," the spirit said. "Humanity will be given what it needs for healing, but it must choose."

"But," Kidwell started but failed to finish as reality shifted once again. The light was gone, and she no longer hovered above the floor. She opened her eyes to stare at the wood and earthen ceiling above her. A deep lethargy filled her, and she felt incapable of moving even her eyes. She lie unmoving, rattling thoughts seeking some form of clarity. All sense of time had deserted her. Had it been moments or hours she floated in the presence of eternity?

Finally, in her line of vision, a boot appeared on the top rail above her. She saw the face of a young man looking anxiously down at her. The sight of another person rooted her back in the world. He hurried, jumping the last few feet and kneeling beside her.

"You okay, lady?" He looked around. "Where are the others? I heard voices, and," he glanced around the kiva, mystified, "I could have sworn I saw light."

A laugh broke Kidwell's lethargy. She felt wonderful, truly alive. "You did," she said. *I'm supposed to 'tell all,'* she thought. *I guess this is a good place to start.*

Sometime during her story, the young man dropped from a kneeling position to a seat in the dirt, too weakened by shock to remain upright. He would be the first, the first to join the cause.

Chapter Two

The Mosque

Aisha looked beyond the yellow crime scene tape to the defaced walls of the mosque. For five years, she had lived and taught at Prairie Land University, a place many would find an odd home for an Iraqi artist, and a woman at that. In five years, it was her first visit to the mosque, to the local sanctuary for the religion of her childhood.

"Death to all rag-heads," was sprawled in bright orange spray paint across the plaster wall beside the carved wood doors of the entrance.

In many ways, Aisha felt safer in Amber, Texas, than she had in many of the places and lands she had once called home. Safety had not been the norm for Aisha during much of her childhood. Her father had opposed the ambitious Saddam Hussein. Her beloved father disappeared one night. The family fled to Turkey, just as her father had arranged, already knowing the danger to his life. They never found the body, but an eyewitness contacted the family, telling of the single shot to the head that had ended her father's life.

Safety had not been common in Aisha's life. As refugees in Turkey, she and her family had known hunger, cold, and fear during the long wait for immigration to the U.S. She fought for her own place in a new culture and experienced a difficult and relatively brief marriage to a man who loved the novelty of an Arab wife but lacked the motivation to understand her. She was glad. Danger had pushed her into herself, caused her to dive into the depths of her soul. It made her as an artist. It made her as a woman. She could not imagine the superficial life of someone who lived constantly with the illusion of safety.

Not that Aisha chose danger and insecurity; quite the opposite. Hence the move to Amber and a tenure-track teaching position. She just knew danger had a way of finding her anyway, and she had chosen long ago not live in fear of its next encroachment.

Neither fear nor dread brought her to a crime scene where people from her new home had leveled an attack against the people of her origin. When she heard the story on the evening news the night before, she was amazed at the wave of emotion she felt, not at the sight of vandalism, but at the sight of a symbol of that belief system in which she no longer participated but which would always be a part of her.

The familiar shape of a mosque triggered a flash of memory of kissing her grandmother's hand, a sign of respect for her as an elder. As the newscaster spoke of the violence against those who followed the Prophet, she looked at the tattoo on her own hand, a duplicate of the one on her grandmother's hand.

"What is it, Grandmother?" she'd asked as a child.

"A beauty mark, my sweet," the woman had answered, giving her granddaughter a gentle smile. Years later, she would realize that the tattoo had been a means of distinguishing herself from the other women when her grandmother had been young. It took creativity to get one's self noticed when young women were covered head-to-toe except for their eyes and hands.

The traditional use of a Hijab did not contain Aisha's life, but she valued her tattoo. It was not used to attract the attention of men, but instead was a reminder of her heritage, the past, and traditions of her family and her people. She touched the skin of the tattoo, caressing her own hand. The motion expressed the love she felt for her late grandmother. Thinking of how her grandmother had used the tattoo to attract a husband made Aisha appreciate that she lived in simpler times. That led her to pleasant memories of the man who was the gift in her life. Greg's poetry stirred her body as well as her soul, and he was the first man capable of comprehending the compulsion, the life-consuming passion of her art. She shook the thought from her head. There was a deep conviction that this day was not about their love, as much as that meant to her.

A deep sigh, triggered by an old and deep sadness, left Aisha feeling tired yet purged. She looked out the open truck window, not at the defaced mosque, but at the walled garden beside it. The stucco wall had been spared in the vandal's attack, and she could see greenness in the shadow beyond. No crime scene tape blocked the entrance, and Aisha felt a calling, similar to the compulsion that awoke her that morning, driving her to visit the defaced mosque. She rolled up the window and stepped out onto the street, locking her truck before walking toward the garden. As she moved, she felt an excitement so intense that she found it difficult to breathe. She knew of no reason for that level of excitement, but there it was nonetheless.

As she stepped through the open archway, the world shifted. From that moment on, her sense of reality would never be the same.

⚜ ⚜ ⚜ ⚜

The smell of the desert greeted Aisha, taking her to a place she had not visited since childhood. There was no sign of the lush green garden she had seen through the archway. For that matter, there was no sign of the archway. She looked down from where she hovered several feet above the desert floor, only to see her familiar physical body lying face down in the sand. The fear Aisha thought she should be feeling was not there. Instead, there was a deep sense of peace. A desert breeze blew across her face. It drew her attention from her body below, and when she looked ahead, she was no longer hovering above the ground. Aisha walked through the sand, directing her steps toward a traditional Bedouin tent she saw about a hundred yards away. A man and a woman were seated on a rug in the shade of a handful of palm trees. Both wore traditional Arab dress and were looking her direction and smiling with welcome. The woman's face was not covered, and Aisha loved the rebellious challenge mixed with the smile in the woman's expression. As she drew closer, the woman was the first to speak.

"And so, you have come, dear Aisha," she called, rising to hold out her hands to Aisha.

Aisha took the proffered grasp in her own hands. The touch felt wonderful.

"You know my name, but I don't know you," Aisha responded.

The woman reached to brush a strand of hair from Aisha's eyes. The touch felt comforting.

"Your soul knows me, recognizes me. Perhaps a

name would help. I am Khadija," the woman answered.

Aisha fell silent as she realized who stood before her. Here stood the first wife and cherished confidant of the Prophet himself. She knew not the boundaries of this reality. "Are you truly…?"

The woman laughed. "I am a messenger sent to help my husband."

Suddenly, a man stood beside the two women. Aisha turned to face him, and she felt awe encapsulated inside a deep peacefulness. He playfully shook a finger at her.

"Do not do that," he said with a smile. "I am just a man who could have done nothing without the help of Allah and my wise wife. How people ever came to worship me is a complete mystery."

Aisha's face reflected her pleasure. She liked him.

"Sit," he said. "We have a cool drink and fruit."

They all took their place on the carpet, and Aisha enjoyed the smell of a desert breeze blowing over the water of the small spring that nurtured the grove of palms. The woman poured drinks from an earthen jar into earthen cups. Aisha did not recognize the taste of the juice blend she drank. She only knew that it was wonderful. She wondered briefly if the food and drink were real, and then contemplated that she no longer felt certain of the definition of reality.

"Why am I here?" Aisha asked.

"Because you are the one who listened to the call. Because only a woman can bear this burden. Because this is the task that you must accept," the man answered.

"Why—"

The man raised his hand, halting Aisha's question. "You will know what you need to know when you need to know it."

Aisha felt fingers gently wrap around her elbow. The woman leaned forward, touching her arm. "Listen," the woman said.

"It is time for a healing," the man said. Aisha stifled her questions. "You must tell all who will listen that the Scimitar has no edge."

"The Scimitar has no edge?" Aisha repeated, confused.

"Yes, and you must wait for your ally. To find her, you must create this image." The man waved his hand, and Aisha saw a scene flash before her eyes. It was a pair of mountains with a distinctive shape. She knew that the image was burned in her mind, and her hand itched to put it on canvas. "Your ally will speak of hermits."

"I'll remember," Aisha answered.

"Trust your own heart and mind. If it feels right, it is," the man said. "If it feels wrong, it is. Do not ignore that knowledge."

"I'll remember," Aisha said.

Aisha felt the man's gentleness to the depth of her being. "We give you much responsibility, my daughter. I remember that burden. Never forget that you are not alone."

"Is this the one?" a voice behind Aisha asked. "The one tasked with fixing my foolishness?"

Aisha turned to see a stern-faced man with a long, grey beard and dressed in a dark robe.

"Welcome, Grandfather Abraham," the man said. "Join us."

The man sat, taking a freshly filled cup from the woman. He faced Aisha. "For whatever you can do, I am grateful," he said.

They all sat in comfortable silence, enjoying the cool drink, sweet figs, and the smell and feel of water and desert. Aisha was not sure of the point at which her soul slipped quietly back into her body.

❧ ❧ ❧ ❧

"Dear Allah, please, nothing more," Aisha heard and looked up to see the tear-filled eyes of a dark-skinned young man. He gasped. "Thank Allah, you're not dead. I was afraid the vandals had returned and killed someone."

Aisha sat up from where she was sprawled on the ground. She was just inside the archway to the garden, and she saw the green and mixed colors of trees and flowers around her.

"I'm all right," she answered, rising to her feet with the young man's help.

"What happened?" he asked.

Aisha looked at him long and hard. She decided that this was as good a place as any to start sharing her story. He would become the second to follow the cause, the cause championed by two allies.

Chapter Three

The Search

Kidwell could feel more than see Anna waiting behind her. Her lover sat anxiously on the edge of the recliner that served as the reading chair in their shared office. Anna held a throw pillow tightly to her and rocked subtly back and forth. Kidwell turned from the computer screen and smiled wryly at Anna.

"Sweetheart, this is hard enough to do without feeling your gaze boring into the back of my head," Kidwell said.

Anna laughed as she stood, throwing the pillow onto the recliner. She walked directly behind Kidwell and put her arms around the sitting woman.

"Ah, that's better," Kidwell said as she turned back to the computer screen.

"This must be terrifying for you," Anna said.

"For us both, apparently," Kidwell answered.

Anna laughed, and placed a kiss on the top of her lover's head. "I'm here for you, my love."

Having Anna's warmth close to her did help far more than Kidwell expected. Anna was right. Writing the email was one of the hardest things she'd ever had to do. She and Anna pasted every screen name they could find into the "blind copy to" box with Anna's screen name the only one posted in the "send to" box. Kidwell tried not to think of the faces that went with many of those screen names. A few would simply accept her message, even feel joy at the experience she'd had. Others had known her for years as a levelheaded, reliable Naval officer. Only once in her Navy career had she risked telling anyone of her psychic experiences. That once had put her career on the line, but it was worth it. She had saved lives and would have saved more if they had fully listened to her. No official record mentioned the warning she'd issued, but she knew the Bronze Star on her record was there because of it, no matter what the official account said. Kidwell knew that when she hit "send," she would be losing the respect and, perhaps, the friendship of people with whom she'd served and whom she'd grown to love and respect.

No matter, Kidwell thought. It must be done. She took a deep breath and placed her hands on the computer keys as she read what she had composed. Anna stayed behind her, kneading gently at Kidwell's tense neck and shoulder muscles. Kidwell read from the beginning, returning her mind to the subject at hand.

"To everyone I know –

"This is quite possibly the most difficult email I've ever written. I have a message…a message that's supposed to go to the whole world. For those of you who don't automatically delete this email, thinking as you do so that CDR Brown's going totally nutty, I ask you to forward this to others. There's no promise of riches if you send this to five people nor a fear of curses if you don't. Just do what you think is right.

"Last week, I went to a place that is holy to me, the Ceremonial Cave at Bandelier National Monument.

When I entered the kiva, something magical happened. I don't know if it was a vision, or reality, or a moment of insanity, but I know I have to do what I was instructed to do. It's hard to describe what happened, so I won't even try. Know that I conversed with White Buffalo Calf Woman and Jesus, and I was told to 'tell all' a simple message. It makes no sense to me, but I'll do it. Here 'tis, folks. The simple message was:

"Tell all, Desert Lightning has no power.

"That's it, and I won't bother you all any more, for now, anyway. Thank you for having the patience to read my message.

– "Kidwell Brown, CDR, USN (ret)"

Kidwell turned to Anna, who was reading from where she stood behind the desk chair. "What do you think?"

Anna smiled and touched Kidwell's face. "Do it."

"You know this will affect you as well. God knows how people will react."

Anna shook her head and rolled her eyes. "Remember when you finally moved to New Mexico."

Kidwell laughed. "You mean three years after I knew I was supposed to come here."

"Yes."

"Three miserable, lonely years."

"Yes, and I was here waiting for you all that time."

Kidwell blinked away the tears in her eyes and turned back to the computer. She hit "send" and the email disappeared into cyberspace.

"Done," Kidwell said.

"Good, now we can get on with our day."

"Aren't you anxious about what will happen?" Kidwell asked.

"I'm more eager to start our trip to Amber so we can 'meet your ally,'" Anna answered. "The travel trailer's ready and our bags are packed. Are we still supposed to meet Robert when we get to Amber?"

"Yes." Kidwell turned pensive as she remembered the young man whom she'd met in the kiva cave. He had helped her up from the dirt floor and listened to her story, and then he'd handed her another miracle. He was a student at Prairie Land University, the land of the Lone Wolf, the place where she was to seek her ally. He had given her the clue she needed for her next step.

"Let's go then," Kidwell said as she stood.

Anna gave her lover the smile of girlish excitement that made Kidwell's heart swell with love and joy. "We're going to the ranch museum that young student told us about, aren't we?"

"Of course."

"Shopping at the mall?" Anna asked

"Of course."

"What else?"

Kidwell shrugged. "Look for an ally, whatever that means."

Anna's eyes flashed. "It means mystery and adventure."

Kidwell's left eyebrow rose skeptically, and for an instant, she looked the no-nonsense Naval officer.

"Aye, yi, yi," Anna said. "How can someone have a soul with such wings and still spend so much time tied to the earth?"

Kidwell looked shyly at the lover who knew her so well. She took Anna's hand and raised it to her lips. "At least I have someone who reminds me when it's time to fly."

The crowd milled amicably, as crowds always mill in the civilized environment of an art opening. Aisha sipped at the wine Greg handed her earlier. She smiled and nodded at the people who paused to tell her how much they loved her new work. She was not afflicted with the terror that so often immobilized artists as they waited for the approval or the rejection of their public. Approval felt pleasant, but criticism was only mildly annoying for her. Aisha painted because something inside whined and begged, scratched and clawed for release. When that creative creature remained fed and happy, her soul was at peace. The art openings and the patrons simply provided the sales that helped feed the body, educate her daughter, and pay for the paint and canvas. Even that mattered little. Her teaching assured survival.

Tonight's opening was unusual. Aisha reminded herself to focus on to the three-piece mural that was the centerpiece for the show. Arab women walked across a Texas sky, jars balanced gracefully upon their heads. Below them, a mixed landscape of Southwest mesas and Iraqi desert blended into a world of its own, much as Aisha herself had managed to do. Aisha divided her time between conversation with those who paused to view the work, and frequent glances toward the humblest piece in her show. The painting was small, one that had only taken a few hours for her to complete. Unlike her other art, it was a simple landscape, distinct only because of her use of color and light to enhance what she saw. The twin mountains in the painting were an unusual shape, rounded with distinct cliff faces rather than the usual series of pointed peaks.

Greg stood near the simple painting, just as she had asked him to do. She made eye contact with her man, and he smiled and nodded, letting her know that he was where she needed him to be. Greg looked away, and she followed his gaze to two women walking the edge of the gallery, pausing to look at each painting. They were not a part of the Texas Panhandle's usual crowd of art connoisseurs, mostly the wives of Texas cattlemen and oil barons looking for a way to spend their husband's money. The local rich mixed with a handful of fellow artists there either to support Aisha or to check out the competition. These two were different, tourists perhaps. The women walked arm-in-arm, leaning companionably against each other as they paused to look at the paintings. The two talked and laughed together. They were obviously comfortable in each other's company. The dark-haired *chicana* had a golden laugh that could be heard from across the room, while the shorter woman with the salt-and-pepper brown hair had a quieter presence, but a smile as contagious as her partner's laughter. At one point, the Hispanic woman glanced over her shoulder, and saw Aisha's tiny landscape from across the room. Her eyes widened, and she grasped the sleeve her of her companion's shirt. They were too distant for Aisha to hear the words, but Aisha could see the intensity of their reaction as both women saw the painting. They walked directly to the landscape, where Greg already waited, standing as inconspicuously as he could near the painting. Luckily, Aisha was not engaged in conversation at that moment, and she crossed the room toward the group.

"Do you see it, *Querida?*" the Hispanic woman

asked. "It's our mountains."

"So you like Aisha Sudda's landscape?" Greg asked. "It's not like her other work."

"When was she at Hermit's Peak?" the shorter woman asked.

Aisha fought for breath. "Did you say Hermit's Peak?" she asked.

The two women turned to face the artist. "Yes," the shorter woman answered. "You painted it almost exactly as we see it from our kitchen window."

Aisha looked into the woman's eyes. For a moment, she felt lost, unreal. She saw a similar feeling reflected in the other woman's face.

"Then you must be my ally," Aisha said.

The other woman went pale. Without a word, she stepped close and wrapped Aisha in the embrace of a long-lost sister. Aisha found herself returning the hug, tears stinging at her eyes.

"Thank God I'm not alone in this," the woman said.

Aisha expressed her agreement by strengthening the embrace.

Chapter Four

The Warning

Anna placed her key in the door and sighed exhaustedly. Kidwell was close behind her, each of them laden with luggage. Anna turned the key, and they entered the living room of their mountain home.

"It was a great trip, but it's even better to get home," Kidwell said as she dropped her burdens in the middle of the living room floor. She turned to go back outside and retrieve the package that had been too precious to carry with the other luggage. Wrapped in brown paper and resting on the floorboard of their Jeep was Aisha's painting of Hermit's Peak. It had been a gift from Aisha and Greg, another sign of the depth of friendship that had grown in just two short days.

"I'll get Aisha's painting," Kidwell said.

"Leave the trailer where it is. We can back it into the shed and unhitch it in the morning," Anna responded.

When Kidwell returned, Anna met her at the door.

"There's a message on the answering machine for you," Anna said.

"Who from?"

"A Tom Franconi."

A smile lit Kidwell's tired face. "Senior Chief

Tom Franconi? Heck, it's probably Master Chief by now. What the heck does he want?"

"He's here, and he wants to see you."

"Here?"

"Yes, here," Anna responded, tired and increasingly annoyed. "He's staying at the Plaza Hotel in town and wants you to call him."

Kidwell glanced at the wall clock. "Too late tonight."

"Listen to the message. He wants you to call as soon as you get home, and he doesn't sound like a man to be ignored."

"No shit," Kidwell responded. "I've seen admirals who'd rather eat dog food than cross Tom Franconi. You remember me telling you about Tom."

A worried crease appeared on Anna's forehead. "What do you suppose he wants? Isn't he still in Norfolk?"

"That's the last I'd heard. He's a man of the sea, tried and true. I can't see him taking a vacation in the mountains."

Anna handed Kidwell the cordless phone and a piece of paper with a number scrawled across it. "Call," she commanded.

Kidwell knew when to obey an order.

❧ ❧ ❧ ❧

"Geeze, you do this for fun?" Master Chief Tom Franconi panted as he paused on a particularly steep portion of the trail.

"Every chance we get," Kidwell answered, breathing hard but not suffering as much as her companion. "Take it easy, Tom. It's the altitude. Takes a while for the lungs to adjust. If you hadn't already been in the area for a couple of days, I wouldn't have suggested this hike. Don't want an old salt like you getting altitude sickness."

"So why'd you drag this sea dog up here anyway?"

"You said you wanted a private place to talk."

Tom looked at the woods surrounding them. They hadn't seen another soul since they left the trailhead an hour earlier. "Yeah, I'd say this is pretty private."

"So, when you going to tell me what brought you here?"

"If you'll have enough mercy to find us a place to sit for a while, we can talk now."

Kidwell looked up the trail. She remembered a high meadow where she and Anna had camped once. It was less than a quarter mile up the trail.

"If you can make it a little farther, there's a great place where we can stop for lunch." After seeing the reaction of the fearless Master Chief when a green snake had slithered across the trail, Kidwell decided not to tell the story of the meadow. When she and Anna camped there, a bull elk had walked into the meadow and bugled a warning to his herd while standing just a few feet from their tent. They'd stayed in the tent, but unzipped the window in time to see the backside of the elk as he crashed his way back into the woods. He could just have easily decided to defend his herd from the invasive presence of a tent and both women knew it. The copper taste of fear mingled with the relief of disaster avoided. They'd given up on sleep and played cards under the camp lantern until the wee hours of the morning.

Tom took a seat on a fallen log as Kidwell spread

her poncho to use as a ground cloth. Tom drank deeply from his water bottle, and Kidwell emptied the picnic lunch from her daypack.

"Okay, Tom. Time to talk and that's an order."

Tom smiled slyly. "Since when have you known a Master Chief worth his salt who obeyed an order without questioning it?"

"You're right. Exercise in futility. So, how about telling a friend why you're here?"

"I got a message for you, but first there's something I've wanted to tell you ever since you retired."

"Shoot."

"I think all that 'don't ask, don't tell' stuff was total bullshit. It was an honor to serve with you, Commander. I know you retired as soon as you could 'cause of that stuff, and it was the Navy's loss, and I'm sorry for it."

Kidwell blinked back tears. It was an unexpected compliment from a man whose opinion she valued. "Tom, that means a great deal to me."

"'Nuff said," Tom answered and then cleared his throat. It was the closest Kidwell had ever seen the hard-boiled sailor come to sentimentality. "Like I said, I'm supposed to ask you a question and then give you a message."

"Who sent you?"

"No problem answering that. He said to tell you. Admiral O'Hare sent me."

Kidwell's breath caught in her throat. Admiral O'Hare was a man she respected, loved, and feared.

"Question first, I guess," Kidwell said.

"Yep. Where'd you hear about Desert Lightning?"

Kidwell blushed. "God, Tom, of all the people I know, you're going to be a tough one to tell this story."

"I'm the one who's asking. Better start talking,

Commander."

It had taken less courage to walk into a burning compartment on the USS Montezuma during Desert Storm than it took to tell of her vision to this hard-boiled sailor. Tom had been there that day too. Remembering that helped. They'd never discussed that day or the unusual role she played in it, but she knew Tom remembered. Perhaps that would help him understand, even believe.

Kidwell took a deep breath and told him everything about her experience in the kiva cave. She told him of the nonsensical message to "tell all desert lightning has no power." She told him of White Buffalo Calf Woman (whom she had to explain) and of Jesus. She told it all.

The old salt listened silently, puffing at the blackened and worn pipe he'd smoked for as long as she had known him. When she was done, he said nothing for a very long time.

"It was kinda like that day on the Montezuma, wasn't it?"

"Yeah, in a way," Kidwell answered.

The Master Chief looked hard at the woman. "You were right that day."

"Yes, I was," she answered.

"The Admiral wishes he'd listened."

The two veterans sat in silence, each lost in their remembering.

❧ ❧❧ ❧

Lieutenant Kidwell Brown poured a cup of nearly lethal coffee from the urn in the ship's galley. She chose a seat beside the Associated Press photographer who was half the reason she found herself the only woman on board the USS Montezuma.

"Hey, Frank," she said to the bearded veteran of the journalism wars.

"Hey," the man answered, looking up from the pulp western he'd borrowed from the ship's library. "How's our star reporter?"

"Stopped puking, but he's still moaning like a four-year-old with a belly ache."

"How the hell did you end up with this babysitting job?" the photographer asked.

"Luck of the draw. How about you? How did you end up riding shotgun with the little bastard?"

"He demanded to come to the Gulf War. Guess he's a nephew to one of the muckity mucks. They didn't give me an option. Told me to watch his ass." The man placed the paperback face down on the table and cleared his throat. "Actually, Kidwell, it's me you can blame for the babysitting job. I requested you. Figured you were the only PAO I knew who could keep the kid in line without strangling him."

"Gee, thanks." Kidwell answered. "At least we both get a few days of cushy duty. Kid's too sea-sick to make us follow him around."

"Yeah, and I'm getting some good candid shots of the crew. He'll still be able to make a story out of it."

"Damn thing is he can really write."

"Grow up a bit, and I think he'll make a real, live journalist."

"Ever worked with Woodson?"

"Nope, but I hear he can be a son-of-a-bitch."

"I'll keep my opinion to myself," Kidwell responded.

"I can read between the lines."

Kidwell took a sip of her coffee and looked into the dark liquid. "Sometimes I think I'm not a real sailor. I think this stuff sucks."

The photographer reached for her cup and looked at the fluid. "If it wouldn't discolor the paper, I bet I could use it as a fixing solution in the darkroom."

"Wonder if that's what set off the kid's stomach."

"More like fear and his first time at sea."

Kidwell lifted her nearly full cup and rose from her seat. "Think I'll go to the admin office and take a look at their command history. Might as well be of some use while I'm here."

Kidwell set her cup in the slotted tray where the galley staff retrieved dishes for washing. The slots kept the cups and glasses from shifting when the ship rolled with the waves or made a drastic change of course. She left the galley and proceeded down the passageway and then down a ladder leading to the next deck where she would find the administrative offices. The ensign assigned duties as command public affairs officer had greeted her fresh off the chopper when she arrived along with the AP journalist and photographer to whom she was assigned as escort. She was doing her best to teach the enthusiastic young officer all she could during her few days on board the cruiser. She saw that he had potential and had agreed to provide one of his officer interviews for his application for a 1650 designator (restricted line—public affairs).

Kidwell slid down the ladder, using the technique common among shipboard crews. She wasn't as practiced as those with full-time shipboard duty, but the act, simple as it was, reminded her that she was truly a part of the U.S. Navy. The descent down the ladder included a sensation of cold. Kidwell noticed, but thought little of it. The complexity of equipment and environments on the ship could create drastic changes in temperature. As she entered a quiet and slightly darker part of the passageway, she saw an officer standing before her. She didn't know him. That was no surprise, considering the size of the ship's company. But as she walked toward the man, something puzzled her. It took her a moment to realize the cause. The uniform wasn't quite right. They were a style of khakis Kidwell had never worn. To her knowledge, the Navy hadn't used shoulder boards on khaki jackets since World War II, possibly Korea. *What the heck?* Kidwell thought as she walked closer to the man, a Lieutenant Commander.

"I have a message," the man said when she was just a few feet from him. "For my Little John…for John O'Hare."

This was odd indeed, Kidwell thought. What a strange way to refer to the ship's captain.

"If you call him Little John, you must be one of the bravest men on this ship," Kidwell said.

"First, tell him I heard everything he said all those times under the big oak. If I could have answered, I would have told him 'yes.' Every time, I would have said 'yes.'"

"Is this some kind of code? Who are you?"

"Next, and this is very important, tell him to change course thirty degrees to starboard."

"You have to be kidding. A visiting junior officer telling the captain to change course. If I'm lucky, all I'll get is a good laugh."

The man disappeared like an autumn mist. Just before her eyes ceased to see him, a part of Kidwell's mind noted the nametag over his left jacket pocket.

Kidwell held her breath. The passageway warmed as the man departed. Finally, she exhaled, collecting her thoughts and feelings. She knew without a doubt that she'd just conversed with the dead. She wasn't frightened. It wasn't the first time. The talent was passed down in the women of her family. Her first experience had been when she was five, not long after her grandfather died. His spirit had paid her a visit. When she told her mother, the woman's calm and matter-of-fact reaction had set the tone for Kidwell's feelings toward such experiences. They were just a part of life. Something those with the talent dealt with the same as some dealt with the ability to sing or an eye for color. Not all spirits were well intended (human nature didn't appear to change even after death), but Kidwell's mother taught her daughter how to be discerning about the spirits she encountered. The occurrences had been infrequent and something she would never talk about with her Navy colleagues. The silent acceptance of her lesbianism was a fairly common experience for gay and lesbian sailors and officers, but she knew of no one who dared acknowledge any psychic ability.

Today, Kidwell would put it to the test. She had a message for the Captain, and she knew it must be delivered.

"When the spirits speak, it's usually something that matters," her mother had said. Kidwell remembered. She closed her eyes, and she saw the Celtic green of her mother's eyes, another gene passed down from the holy women who had been their ancestors.

Kidwell took a deep breath, stood straight and tall and walked in as direct a path as she knew to the ship's bridge. As she walked, her career flashed before her eyes. *Thirteen years before I can retire*, Kidwell thought. She continued her purposeful walk.

Her palms were sweating profusely as she stood in front of the Captain. She had not felt as frightened of a senior officer since her younger years when she'd first enlisted, before receiving her commission.

"Pardon the intrusion, Captain, but I have an urgent message for you."

Captain O'Hare scowled as he looked at the younger officer. "Lieutenant Brown, isn't it?"

"Yes, sir."

"So who sends this message?"

Kidwell swallowed hard. "From…from Lieutenant Commander O'Hare, sir."

"Is this some kind of joke?"

"Wish to hell it were, sir."

Chief Petty Officer Tom Franconi turned from where he stood behind the helmsmen to look at Kidwell with an expression of contained amusement. She cut her gaze subtly toward Franconi and gave him an "eat shit and die" look.

The Captain was anything but amused. "What is this urgent message?"

"Commander O'Hare had two messages," she answered.

"The first?"

"He said to tell…to tell his Little John that he heard everything he said under the big oak, and, if he could have answered, he would have told you 'yes.'"

The Captain went deathly pale. "And the second?"

"Change course thirty degrees to starboard."

The Captain sat in total silence. Kidwell waited only a few seconds for his reaction, but it felt like an eternity.

"Chief Franconi."

"Aye, sir."

"Please escort Lieutenant Brown to sickbay."

"Aye, sir."

The Captain turned to Kidwell. "I hope you'll understand if I request an examination for you."

"Aye, sir. Psychological?"

"Of course," the Captain answered. "Want out of the Navy, Lieutenant?"

"No, sir," Kidwell answered, standing at attention and angry at the tears she blinked from her eyes.

"Follow me, Lieutenant," Franconi said.

Kidwell did a left face and followed the Chief as instructed. Just before they left the bridge, she heard the captain give the order for all ahead slow.

"All ahead slow, aye," was the response. Kidwell heard the bells that let her know the command had been issued to the engine room deep in the bowels of the ship.

It would be enough, but just barely.

As they descended the ladder from the bridge, Kidwell and Franconi held tightly to the rail, prepared for the change in momentum as the ship slowed.

"You sure know how to end a career with a bang, Lieutenant," Franconi said.

Kidwell compressed her lips, maintaining control of her emotions. "Sometimes a sailor has to do what a sailor has to do."

"No disrespect intended, ma'am. You may be nuts, but you sure got balls," the Chief said.

They walked in silence past the main deck and through a doorway and down into the ship toward sickbay. They were nearly there when they heard a distant explosion. The entire ship shuddered for an instant and then uttered a metallic moan felt throughout her length, as though the vessel were a creature in pain. A shift in momentum for the ship immediately followed the moan. By the feel, Kidwell knew the captain had ordered the ship hard to starboard.

"What was that?" Kidwell asked just before the ship's intercom blared, calling all hands to battle stations.

"Major trouble," the Chief answered.

He looked uncertain, an unaccustomed expression on the face of this confident sailor. They both plastered themselves as close as possible to the bulkhead as officers and men rushed down the passageway, clutching helmets and life-vests, making their way rapidly to pre-designated battle stations. It only lasted a few minutes. The crew knew the drill well.

"I'm not really crazy. You can leave me here. Go where you need to be," Kidwell commanded. Her thoughts were on her "battle station." There were two journalists on this ship, and their safety was her responsibility.

The chief smiled gratefully. "Sounds like a direct order from an officer to me. Guess I better go."

The Chief turned and ran down the passageway, back toward the bridge. That's when they both heard the whoosh and saw a flash of light from an open hatch not far down the passageway. A scream followed, and they turned to see a young sailor, his clothes on fire, rush out of the compartment and into the passageway. Kidwell reached him first, stopping him from running and attempting to force him to the deck. The Chief reached them in a heartbeat and together they were able to force the young man to the floor. The older sailors used the only thing they had handy to snuff the flames, their own bodies. It didn't take long once they got him to the ground. For the most part, their clothing protected them, but Kidwell felt the sear of flesh on her arms and hands. The seaman still wore welder's goggles. They were on his forehead where he'd shoved them when he stopped welding. Kidwell pulled them gently away, knowing their heat must increase his pain.

That's when Kidwell and Franconi turned to the next crisis. Flames licked around the open doorway and into the passageway. The Chief grabbed the hatch first, and Kidwell helped him close and secure the opening.

"That should snuff it," she said.

The Chief looked at the compartment number over the doorway. "I hope to hell it does. We have an ammunition magazine one deck up and directly above."

"Shit," Kidwell responded.

At that moment, she heard movement down the passageway. She looked up to see the photographer with his camera bag slung over one shoulder and dragging the young journalist by the shirtfront with his other hand. The young man was crying and had pissed himself.

A flash of anger carried Kidwell through the next minute. She crossed to the young journalist in two strides and slapped the boy full across the face. His eyes were wide with shock.

"You came here to prove you were a man," she shouted. "So prove it. Pull yourself together and help Frank get this injured sailor up to the main deck." She turned to the photographer. "Frank, can you take care of this boy, get him to a corpsman?"

"Sure, Kidwell. Where will you be?"

"The Chief and I have a fire to see to."

The young journalist did as he was told. He

helped the photographer lift the injured sailor, and the three of them made their way down the passageway walking sideways so they would all three fit with the sailor having one arm around each man's shoulders. The Chief, who knew the whole ship like his own home, was already leading Kidwell to the nearest damage control locker. The Chief grabbed the phone with the direct line to damage control central. Kidwell listened as he reported the situation. Listening to his half of the conversation, she knew they were on their own. Damage control had bigger problems.

"Wonder what caused the fire," Kidwell said. "There wasn't an explosion here."

"There was a work order to repair some damaged shelves in that compartment. He must have been welding. When the ship shuddered and changed course, something flammable must have gotten onto the freshly welded metal."

"Boy must have stayed to put it out."

The Chief nodded approval. "Gonzales, wasn't it?"

"Didn't notice the name on his shirt, but he was Hispanic. I saw that."

As they talked, they took what they needed from the damage control locker. Each donned an Oxygen Breathing Apparatus (OBA) and inserted the canister that, when activated, would turn the device into a re-breather that maintained the oxygen level in their recycled breath. They held helmets, waiting to put them on after the OBA masks were in place. They hooked the fire hose to the wall hydrant and stretched the line. The Chief held the nozzle and eased the valve open gently, avoiding a water hammer that could jerk the nozzle from his grasp. They would have to do without someone to man the valve. There was no third firefighter. Together, they made their way back to the compartment.

"I'll be the access man," Kidwell said. "You're stronger. You can handle the hose alone."

Kidwell activated the canister on her OBA, snugged her mask close to her face, and then secured her helmet. She held the nozzle on the charged hose while the Chief put his gear in place, handing it back to him after he had secured his gear.

"Ready?" the Chief yelled.

"Aye," Kidwell responded.

She stepped in front of him toward the doorway, removing her right glove as she did so. She felt the door with the back of her hand. It was warm but not hot. Good sign but not the best.

"Give me a protective mist," she yelled back at the chief.

He opened the nozzle slightly, creating a mist that enveloped the Lieutenant and the doorway. Kidwell caught her breath at the touch of the cold seawater, but she didn't stop. With the mist protecting her, she opened the latches around the doorway. With the last latch open, she looked over her shoulder to see if the Chief was ready. He nodded in encouragement. She swung the door open, stepping to the side in case flame shot from the opening. Instead, there was a wall of smoke. The chief crouched low and started into the compartment. Kidwell moved to a position behind him as number two nozzle-man. It only took a few minutes to extinguish the fire. When the compartment was cold, they stepped back into the passageway, dragging the hose free of the compartment and into the passageway. Once again, they secured the door to the passageway.

They shut down the valve at the damage control locker and made their way toward the main deck. The fire was out, but smoke still drifted through the area. They dared not remove their OBAs until they were back in clean air.

Once topside, they dropped the OBAs to the deck and re-secured their helmets after the masks had been removed. Now that the adrenaline flow had slowed, she felt the pain of her burns.

"Go to your battle-station, Chief," she commanded. "I better find my journalists and make sure they're still alive and well."

"Lieutenant," Franconi said.

"Yes?"

"We should have changed course thirty degrees to starboard," the hard-boiled Chief said just before he ran toward the ladder to the bridge.

❧ ❧ ❧ ❧

Tom Franconi grabbed a handful of Greek olives from the plastic dish. He'd already finished his ham sandwich and was grazing on the picnic side dishes.

"You know what, Commander?" he asked.

"What?"

"I've seen a lot of things during my twenty-six years in the Navy." He stretched comfortably on the ground cloth and looked seriously at the woman. "But I don't think I've ever seen anyone do anything more courageous than telling Captain O'Hare that his dead daddy wanted him to change course."

Kidwell laughed. "I figured it was the end of my career."

"Why'd you do it?"

Kidwell's head tilted, a confused expression on her face. "Hell, Tom. The Captain's dead daddy was right, wasn't he?"

"Sure was. If we'd maintained speed, we would have plunged right into a minefield. The Montezuma would have sunk that day. I have no doubt of it. As it was, we took one hit and were able to avoid the main body of the field. Admiral O'Hare ever tell you how he knew to give the order for a hard right?"

"No."

"Because you told him to change our course to starboard."

"I'll be damned. He believed me?"

"Yes, he did." The Master Chief paused. "Oh, did he ever tell you what he'd asked his dead daddy when he stood under the big oak?"

"No," Kidwell responded.

"He wanted to know if he made his daddy proud."

Tears teased at the edge of Kidwell's eyes. She cleared her throat before she spoke. "I'm glad I was able to relay the answer."

"The Admiral believes you now, too, Commander, but I have to ask you something again."

"Shoot."

"Where did you learn of Desert Lightning?"

"I told you, Tom. It was a...well...a vision, for lack of a better word."

They sat in silence for some moments.

"Can you tell me about Desert Lightning?" Kidwell asked.

The Master Chief just looked at her sternly.

"I didn't think so," Kidwell responded.

Franconi cleared his throat, and Kidwell could tell from his body language that he was about to carry out an order. He sat straight and tall, his legs crossed in front of him.

"The Admiral figured it was likely to be something like the day when his daddy talked to you. Commander, you could be in danger. I can't tell you any more than that."

There was a flow of ice through Kidwell's veins. She remembered the sensation, but had hoped never to feel it again. It came only when there was real and visceral danger. The confusion of emotion simply went somewhere else, leaving her ready to deal with a crisis with cold clarity.

"Since you can't tell me about Desert Lightning, I'm assuming the danger could come from spooks or some other bunch of our own folks," Kidwell said.

Franconi leaned close to her. Despite their remote privacy, he felt the need to whisper. "Kidwell," he used her name for the first time, "These days, sometimes it's really hard to know who the 'good guys' are. Be glad you're out of it."

"Doesn't look like I am," Kidwell responded.

"Damn if you're not right." The Master Chief leaned back to a position as close as he could get to attention while sitting cross-legged in the woods. "I have one more message from the Admiral."

"Yes?"

"He wanted me to give you a code phrase. If you get a message – a call, email, telegram – anything with that code phrase from either the Admiral or me, head for the woods."

"Go into hiding?"

"Damn right! You and Anna both. The Admiral said he and his son went backpacking with you, and he figures the two of you could do a pretty good job of getting yourself lost."

"When do we come back?"

"Admiral said you'd probably need to go to some backwoods town for supplies every few weeks. Have Anna call him. She's supposed to be the daughter of his college buddy Hector. He'll find a way to let you know if it's safe to come home. If you can't reach him, try me. Same drill."

"What's the code phrase?"

"Thirty degrees to starboard."

Chapter Five

The Matrix

The night breathed with the gentleness of a world asleep. Kidwell awoke, growing to consciousness with an awareness of the comforting warmth of Anna curled next to her, their bodies wrapped in a matching "S," fitting together like pieces of a jigsaw puzzle. It had been the same comforting sensation that had sent her into the peacefulness of sleep just a few hours earlier. She lay in the darkness, wondering what had awakened her. With the knowledge that comes with habitual intimacy, she knew that Anna lay awake as well.

"Do you hear something?" Anna asked.

"I'm not sure," Kidwell answered. There was a hint of music in her mind more than her ears. She wasn't sure if it had been from the physical reality or from her dreams.

"Maybe Greg was playing his flute," Anna said.

Aisha and Greg had been living in the second bedroom of Kidwell and Anna's forest home for several days. Kidwell had called Aisha after meeting with Tom Franconi. When Kidwell told Anna of the warning Franconi had given, the two of them made plans. Neither woman was a stranger to the woods. They had everything they needed – horses, camping equipment, emergency medical supplies – to do as the

Admiral instructed should his call come. They would be ready. As they talked, a new wrinkle arose—their allies. Could the threat extend to them? When Kidwell called, Aisha had answered the phone before it finished the first ring.

"There's no need to invite us," Aisha said.

Kidwell paused, surprised. "What?"

"Weren't you calling us to invite us to stay at your house?"

"Yes."

"I had another vision. Khadija – you remember, Mohammed's first wife – told me to go to my ally, to go to the mountains."

"Can you leave?"

"I'm not teaching this summer, and Greg has been scheduled to do a study of small-diameter trees on forestry land for a long time. He can work there. Is there a place where I can paint?"

"Yeah, there's good light in our office, or perhaps even in the barn. The tack room is large, pretty good light, and you'd have privacy."

"We've already canceled our other commitments. Is tomorrow too soon?"

Kidwell laughed. "No. Bring your sleeping bags and any personal camping equipment you need."

"In my vision, the Prophet's wife said to be ready to go to the wilderness."

"I heard something similar, but it came from a Master Chief."

"What?"

"I'll explain when you get here."

As she and Anna lay in the darkness, Kidwell's thoughts returned to the present. It could have been Greg's Choctaw flute. Since their guests had arrived,

Kidwell and Anna had grown accustomed to its mystical melodies. He played it almost every evening. It could have been Greg's flute, but it was not. She was sure of that.

The music returned, not just the flute but the drum as well, and behind that, something more, something she had no clue how to explain or understand. It was the essence of music, sounds that enlivened that part of the soul that motivated humanity to make music, to listen to music, to understand music.

"You hear that?" Kidwell asked.

"I hear it, but I don't understand it," Anna answered.

The two women donned bathrobes and hurried from the bedroom to go down the stairs and into the living room. As soon as they stepped out the bedroom door and onto the open stairway, they saw Aisha and Greg in the living room, wearing bathrobes as well and looking tousled and sleepy.

"You hear it too?" Greg asked, looking up at the two women.

"If we're crazy, at least we're all crazy together," Kidwell said.

Anna grasped Kidwell's shoulders from behind and shook her gently. "You have a wonderful gift. Why must you always wonder if it's insanity?"

As the women reached the living room, the four companions stood looking at each other. Without planning to do so, they arranged themselves in a circle. Once in place, a sensation as sure as electric current ran through them all, joining them in a matrix of energy and emotion. Kidwell felt the now familiar sensation of losing her body. She glanced at Anna and then Greg.

"Welcome to the world of visions," she said just

before the world shifted to another reality for all of them.

Below them, four crumpled figures lay on the floor, arranged in a loose circle.

"That's me," Kidwell felt Anna say. Kidwell's spirit looked to her soulmate, and she would have caught her breath, if her spirit had had breath to catch. It was Anna and then it was not; she saw the flow of the different forms and shapes of the person Anna had been during the many lives they had shared together. As she looked into Anna's ever changing eyes, she saw surprise reflected there and knew that Anna was having a similar experience. Memory flooded through Kidwell. With each new face she saw, the memory of that lifetime returned. At some level, she knew that the memories were a temporary gift, but she savored them like a starving woman seated at a banquet. Together she and Anna had shared flashes of memories from key moments in their shared past, but Kidwell now felt the beautiful enormity of what they had known together. She was vaguely aware of Aisha and Greg, still within their circle, and she knew without being told that they were also lost in the hidden memories of each other. After a length of time that could have been an instant or an eternity, Kidwell had no clue which it was, she saw the many faces of her soulmate join into a single flash of light, and Anna congealed into a glow with only a hint of human form within. As Kidwell saw Anna's transformation, her awareness of their other two companions changed as well. She now saw Aisha and Greg as creatures of light.

The four companions were not alone. When Kidwell could tear a fraction of her attention from Anna, she felt the now familiar presence of White Buffalo

Calf Woman, and she saw another presence, one that she knew without being told was Khadija. They were creatures of light as well, but Kidwell had no difficulty recognizing who they were. Behind them…dear God, behind them was a cauldron of spirits. Kidwell felt she was looking into the infinity of the human spirit.

"You are here. That is good, for we need you to be a part of this matrix, you who must carry the message into the world of earth, wind, fire, and air," White Buffalo Calf Woman said. Kidwell saw, but did not hear the Prophet's wife welcome Aisha in much the same way.

Anna had drifted to a place beside Kidwell. In the habit of their physical forms, the two women reached to hold hands. When their spirits touched, they both cried out with the joy of the sensation. Despite the intensity, they managed to stay connected to the others, avoiding the temptation to be lost in each other.

"Why are we here?" Anna asked.

"The time has come for great balance," White Buffalo Calf Woman said.

"Or great destruction," the Prophet's wife completed.

"We invite you to join the matrix," the being in white said.

"The matrix?" Kidwell asked.

"Enough of humanity, both of spirit and of flesh, has reached balance. They have acquired the ability to connect with the energy of the universe. Together we shall strive to prevent the great destruction," White Buffalo Calf Woman said.

Kidwell saw a press of sprits behind their guides. One spirit reached forward and touched White Buffalo Calf Woman lightly. White Buffalo Calf Woman emitted a flash of pleasure that could best be described as a spiritual laugh.

"They wish to meet you," she said.

"Who?" Kidwell asked.

"If you will allow their touch, you will know," White Buffalo Calf Woman answered.

Anna moved toward the caldron of light that was the matrix of human spirits.

"Anna," Kidwell called.

Her light lover turned to her. "Come, *Querida*. It will be fine."

Kidwell moved to Anna's side, and, in an instant, they were consumed. Kidwell knew one soul and she knew thousands in a moment of time. She saw flashes of vision from the time of their flesh, and she knew who they were. Destruction surrounded them—fire and blood, courage and fear. A Raggedy Ann doll lay in the rubble. She experienced each death as a single unit. There was the woman working at her desk in one moment and a ball of fire falling to the pavement far below in the next; then the fireman rushing up the steps, fighting against the wave of those seeking safety below until the second they were all caught in the crush of rubble, themselves becoming rubble.

They are from the Twin Towers, Kidwell thought, and then she remembered her experience the ill-fated day of September 11, 2001. She had watched the television screen in horror as the buildings fell, and then she had seen what others could not see. Twin beams of purple light flowed from the destruction to the sky above. *The souls*, Kidwell thought. It is the freed souls, and in a moment of emotional confusion, she cried in joy, a fact that had caused her silent guilt in the aftermath of death and destruction.

Kidwell remembered also the vision she had when she joined a Wiccan Samhain circle Halloween week of that year. During a guided meditation, she had been told to walk into the underworld where she would find someone from the other side of death who would have a message for her. The vision was not what she had expected. It was not her father, nor anyone she had known in life who awaited her. It was a single shrouded figure, sitting beside the fire. She had looked inside the hood to see a cauldron of light, a vision she now knew to be a matrix of souls.

"Will you finish what we started?" the hooded figure asked, speaking with one voice and a thousand voices.

"If it does not upset the balance of the universe, I will try," Kidwell answered.

The vision ended, and, until this moment, she had not known what it meant. *It was those lost on 9/11*, Kidwell thought. She also knew her task. From the other side, those souls were fighting for balance in humanity. It was her task, the one she had accepted, to do her part to help from the side of the living.

As soon as it had begun, it was over. The souls retreated, and she and Anna were once again figures of light in the company of their two earthly companions and their two guides.

"Now that you understand, do you still accept the task you were given?" White Buffalo Calf Woman asked Kidwell.

"I will do all I can," Kidwell answered. Anna, Aisha, and Greg added their pledge to the task.

That was when they heard the cacophony below them. Drums, flutes, cymbals, bagpipes, voices, pianos, organs. It was the sound of ceremonies from throughout the world. As spirits of light, the four companions were able to look at the world below where they saw and heard all those who had felt the call to prayer. Only in the freedom of their spiritual selves could they see and comprehend on such a grand scale. They saw groups of souls break away from the matrix and go to the ceremonies below. When the spirits reached the respective groups, they watched as the living people experienced the separation that was now familiar to both Kidwell and Aisha. Their physical forms dropped to the ground and their spirits flew free, still bearing the appearance of their physical selves. As the groups joined their spirit guides and flew toward the matrix, Kidwell noted that a lone spirit remained with the physical forms, watchful and protecting. She glanced below at her own body, and saw the bluish-white of the spirit assigned to their protection.

"Welcome them," White Buffalo Calf Woman commanded.

Kidwell and Anna flew together, joining a small group of spirits from the matrix, to a circle of Diné, gathered in a hogan, sharing smoke and singing with the beating of the drum. As Kidwell and Anna hovered above, the physical forms of all but one of the Diné dropped to the ground, and their astral bodies left to hover above them. Anna and the other spirits welcomed them, offering to serve as their guides. Kidwell turned her attention to the young man below, shaking his companions' physical forms, obviously fighting panic. He had been willing, but his spirit had not been ready. She willed herself to take the appearance of her physical form, although she still hovered four feet above the floor.

"Don't be frightened," Kidwell said. The young

man looked at her. "Your friends have been called to help with an important task. They will return. Stay. Guard their bodies," she commanded.

"I understand," he said, calm returning to his face.

They flew as a group to join the matrix.

The next day, when the four companions were once again conjoined with their physical selves, they would watch the news and learn of worldwide amazement at an inexplicable sighting of Northern Lights so strong that eyewitnesses saw it from almost the entire globe, excluding only the southern-most portions of the world. It was an odd comfort to know that the matrix had existed at some level in the physical world.

For tonight, they simply welcomed the work they must share with humanity's spiritually enlightened. Although Kidwell could not have told anyone how she knew, she felt certain that their work that night was a fight for the very survival of humanity, for the species to evolve into what it could be.

The four companions did their part in the matrix. They joined the others in re-weaving reality.

Chapter Six

Desert Lightning

Vice-Admiral John O'Hare sat in his favorite leather recliner at home, having just fought – and lost – the bloodiest battle of his career. It had not been from the deck of a ship nor with small arms at any shore-based command. The battle had been fought and lost in the bowels of the Pentagon, sometimes in the offices, impressive in their rebuilt opulence in the aftermath of 9/11. He had fought Desert Lightning with every ounce of persuasion, every contact he had made during thirty years in the Navy.

Ice clinked against the sides of his glass, two fingers of bourbon now down to less than one. For the most part, the Admiral had avoided the dependence on alcohol that had plagued so many of his shipmates, but tonight he felt the warm numbness of alcohol was well justified. He had fought what he saw as total insanity with everything he had, and it would likely be the end of his career. If he were lucky, he would simply be allowed to retire. Only one other among the high-ranking military officers had been willing to take a similar risk to stop Desert Lightning. General Festus Chandler, Commander, Strategic Command, had gone so far as to call the President, to his face, a delusional idiot. General Chandler had been relieved of his command and was awaiting trial for insubordination. O'Hare would like to think he would have had courage equal to Chandler's, but he had not had the opportunity. His pleas had been directed to the Secretary of the Navy. O'Hare had seen understanding in the man's eyes, even agreement. In the end, O'Hare concluded that the Secretary simply lacked Chandler's courage. He would do as he was ordered.

O'Hare had one card left to play. He sat with the phone on the table beside his recliner, his worn and tattered address book on his lap. It was turned to the B's, to Commander Kidwell Brown, USN (ret). He'd been ready to call when he had first come home at midnight after marathon hours of last-minute arguments. He had prayed that wisdom would overcome fervor and that Desert Lightning would become nothing more than a foolish plan never heard of by anyone but high-ranking military officials. His prayer had not been answered. Kidwell Brown was in danger. A lot of people were in danger, but he could do something about Kidwell. As he sat with the phone, preparing to dial the number, he looked up to see his late father standing before him, dressed in the same khakis he had worn when issuing the warning to Kidwell Brown, then Lieutenant Brown, during Desert Storm.

"Not yet, Johnny," the apparition said. "She and her allies still have work to do."

"Daddy?" the Admiral asked.

"I'm still proud of you, son," the ghost said, just before he faded like an evaporating mist. As the vision faded, the man's voice still echoed a few last words of encouragement. "You did what you could."

The Admiral set his glass on the table. He no longer needed a drink. Instead, he cried. For the first time in thirty years, he wept with full abandon. There was relief in his tears. He felt certain that he had done all he could or should do. His daddy had said so.

⁂

Boatswains Mate First Class Gonzales stood at his place beside the helm. The metal of the wheel where his hands touched felt warm and slick from the sweat he'd left there. In a few minutes, the guided missile cruiser that was his current home would launch enough ordnance to destroy the state of New Jersey. It was his job to keep the ship on course. It was not his job to fear the destruction they would cause, to wonder about the people who would feel the wrath of the strike, to question the rightness of their actions. He did that on his own.

Gonzales scratched at the burn scars on his neck, the ones he had incurred during his first tour in the Middle East, during Desert Storm. They always itched when he was nervous. As they steamed full speed ahead, he thought of the Lieutenant who had helped Chief Franconi rescue him that day. There had been rumors on the ship about her. He had heard them as he lay in his bunk in sickbay. His burns had been bad, but they could have been far worse. In the end, they'd decided to treat him onboard ship rather than air evacuating him to a shore-based hospital. He was glad. He had not wanted to leave the Montezuma, especially when she was wounded and might need him. The rumors said that the Lieutenant – a public affairs officer on short-term assignment to the Montezuma – had come to the bridge and boldly instructed the Captain to turn thirty degrees to starboard just minutes before they struck the mine. The helmsman on the bridge told Gonzales that the Captain ordered them to decrease speed, even though he had also sent her to medical to await psychiatric evaluation. If he had not given that order, they would have hit a minefield, not just a single mine.

She had saved the ship. They all knew it. As Gonzales' sweaty hands held the wheel, he wondered where she was. He wondered what she would think of the massive attack that would be launched this day, as Operation Desert Lightning became reality. He wished he could hear what she had to say.

Gonzales could feel the presence of the executive officer in the command chair behind him. The Captain was below in Combat Information Central (CIC). That is where the action would be this day. That is where he would give the order to strike, an effort that would be coordinated with sea, air, and land forces of the U.S. and its allies throughout the Middle East. Gonzales looked at his watch. Three minutes before launch. He had overheard Lieutenant Johnson saying that the cruise missiles they would launch today had a dollar value that, if applied to food, could feed the entire United States for two years. That was their ship alone. Gonzales could not even grasp the bill for every piece of ordnance that would be used that day.

"Steady on, helmsman," the Commander instructed.

"Aye, sir. Steady on," Gonzales responded. He realized that his body language must have been expressing his nervousness.

One minute until launch. Gonzales took a deep breath and concentrated on the wheel and compass that were his primary responsibility right now. No matter what, he knew he would do his job. From the first time he had set foot on a sailing vessel, Gonzales knew his place in the world. He had never married, never really had a home on shore. Bachelor enlisted quarters had always been good enough for him. He had put in far more sea duty than most of his compatriots. He had done so because he always requested sea duty, despite the fact that his reluctance to serve shore-based commands had been part of the reason he had been passed over for Chief. He loved the ships on which he served as though they were home and lover all mingled into one. In a few years, he would face retirement. He already had his boat chosen. When the Navy no longer allowed him at the helm of the big ships, he would be at the helm of his own ship – a twenty-four-foot sailing yacht. He had saved his entire career for that boat, and he intended to operate a commercial sailing business, teaching others about the sea, with a homeport in the Virgin Isles.

Thinking about his boat relaxed Gonzales. Sixty seconds clicked away and he barely noticed. He didn't notice until they were past. Nothing happened. No rush of sound as the missiles left their berths. No slight adjustment of course required to maintain heading despite the sideward thrust on the vessel caused by the power of the firing missiles. Nothing. Gonzales glanced at his fellow crewmembers around the bridge. They shared a confused and nervous look. Gonzales thought he saw his own sense of relief reflected on other faces. He glanced over his shoulder at the executive officer. There was a worried furrow between his eyes. The Commander picked up the command phone by his chair and called CIC.

"Bridge to CIC. This is Commander Stickler. Give me the Captain," he said into the phone. The bridge was silent as every member of the crew held their breath, listening to the Commander's half of the conversation.

"I'm sure he is busy, sailor, but we need to know what the hell is happening." There was a pause. "He's in secured communication with the Admiral?" A smile touched at the corners of the commander's lips. "Has the attack been scrubbed then?"

Another pause. "Well then, God damn it, put someone on the phone who does know something." Another pause. "Lieutenant, what the hell's happening down there?"

A longer pause. "I hear you talking, but the only message I get out of it is that you don't know what's happening. This is your executive officer speaking, Lieutenant. I want answers." Another pause. "Well, that's not good enough." The Commander hung up the phone with such force that Gonzales was afraid it would break.

"Chief Span," the Commander barked to the senior enlisted man on the bridge.

"Aye, sir."

"Go down to CIC and find out what's happening and then report back to me."

"Aye, sir."

The Chief was out the door and down the ladder in a heartbeat. The rest of the bridge crew stared enviously after him. Gonzales did not believe he had ever felt such an intense curiosity.

"Any change of course or speed, sir?" Gonzales asked.

"Did you hear an order for any change, Petty Officer Gonzales?"

"No, sir, but—"

"Then steady on."

There was silence on the bridge. All hands glanced frequently at the doorway, awaiting Chief Span's return. It was less than a half hour before he did appear, but it had seemed like an eternity for everyone.

"It's about time, Chief," the Commander growled. "What's happening?"

"It's…it's unbelievable, Sir."

"Belay the judgment calls and just give me the facts, Chief."

"We fired as planned, sir."

The Commander's entire posture expressed surprise. "Don't bullshit me, Chief."

"I'm not sure. We should have launched exactly as planned."

"Well, Chief, I may be getting a little old and slow, but I know I didn't see one missile leave this vessel."

"That's the point, sir. They didn't."

"Some form of sabotage?" the Commander asked.

"When I was in CIC, they were checking and crossing-checking every possibility, but all systems seem go except for one thing. They won't launch."

"That's not possible."

"Exactly, sir, but that's not everything."

"What else?" the Commander asked.

"It's not just us. Nothing fired," the Chief said.

"Either I'm dreaming or I misunderstood you, Chief."

"Neither, sir. It's true. Reports are coming in from everywhere – Navy, Marines, Army, Air Force – even the Brits and the Aussies. Nothing fired. No missiles, no bombs left bomb bays, no artillery, not even the small arms of the ground troops. Nothing."

"What about the enemy?" the Commander asked.

"Apparently, nothing. No reports of retaliation."

"That's not possible," the Commander said.

"Aye, sir," the Chief responded.

"What do we do now?" the Commander asked.

"Celebrate," Seaman John Johnson said from his post near the navigator.

A wave of laughter rippled across the bridge before the Commander's scowl silenced everyone.

"Well, Seaman Johnson, if the Chief is right, perhaps you should go make that suggestion to the Captain, or better yet, the Admiral," the Commander said.

Seaman Johnson blushed and looked intently at his shoes. Gonzales secretly thought Johnson's suggestion was the best idea he'd heard in a very long time. He'd tell Johnson so when their watch was over.

The ship's intercom blared, and the order was broadcast to stand down from battle stations. The wheel no longer felt slick and sweaty under Gonzales' hands. His ship was safe, and he sighed in relief.

Chapter Seven

Scimitar's Edge

Ambassador Abdul Sassar sat in the plush backseat of the limousine. Framed photographs of his wife, children, and grandchildren rested on the seat beside him. He looked at the photos longingly, blinking back the tears, knowing he must look composed and peaceful when they arrived at the guard post. The photos came from his desk. He had left in their place a sealed letter, explaining that his participation in the day was not a willing act and pleading for protection for his family. His wife had duplicates of the photos or ones very similar with her at home; otherwise, he would not have put them in his briefcase before being escorted to the waiting limo. He would not have wanted to leave his wife without copies of the cherished photos. Within the hour, there would be nothing recognizable left of the frames and photos beside him, just as there would be nothing recognizable left of him.

The Ambassador sat in a plush, comfortable, and highly powerful bomb. He was not there by choice. He was not there because of a belief in a fanatical cause. He was there to protect the people in the photos on the seat beside him. If he had not agreed to take his place in the limousine, part or all of them would have been dead before sundown. The Ambassador picked up the photo of his two favorite grandchildren, five-year-old Karem and seven-year-old Leesha. A shudder ran through his body as he thought of the fate that could have awaited such beautiful children at the hands of cruel and angry men, men who deluded themselves into believing that their cruelty was the righteous wrath of Allah. *Allah protect us from the righteous*, the Ambassador thought.

There was a time when the Ambassador would have said "no" to the terrorists' demands and accepted the bullet to his head, praying for the protection of his family as he died. He looked through the windows of the limo at the all-too-familiar city of Washington, DC, as they drove through the diplomatic district. As he thought ahead to the capitol area and the men and women who waited there, he wondered where his allies for peace had gone. For decades, he had served his country, served Allah, served humanity as best he could. His service had been made possible because he always knew where to find those from the Christian West who shared his vision for peace and balance between their two worlds. Lately, those bridge builders had all-too-frequently joined the ranks of the retired (usually with great reluctance). The younger voices had been silenced in other ways: placed in powerless positions, belittled and blackmailed in the political arena. With great bitterness, he wondered if the powerful weapon disguised as a luxury vehicle might not actually prove to be a gift in the floundering struggle for peace. He prayed not, and he prayed it would be. If he must die, he hoped it would further the cause for peace. He had lived for it. He would prefer to die for it.

"In the hands of Allah," he muttered to himself.

The wild-eyed young man in the driver's seat

looked at the Ambassador through the rear-view mirror. "Did I hear you call on Allah?" the young man said. "What good will that do you? You who have so long served the infidel dogs?" The young man spit on the seat beside him, not caring about the expensive upholstery. The Ambassador smiled humorlessly. It didn't matter. That upholstery would soon be charred remains.

"Allah hears many voices," the Ambassador answered. The young man laughed harshly and spat again in answer.

Although the Ambassador had never seen the young man before rough hands shoved the diplomat into the backseat of the limo, the Ambassador knew him. He had known thousands of young men like him, men full of anger and blame. The hate-mongers preyed on these angry young men, harvesting them regularly to fill their ranks of the violently righteous. In his work at home, he had spent much time fighting those who vehemently protected the refugee camps and social injustices that served as the greenhouse for growing new crop after new crop of angry young men.

"Now you will ride with the Scimitar's Edge," one of his kidnappers had said as they walked to the car.

The driver had rolled down his window and spoken joyously to his fellow terrorist, drunk on the only moment of power he would ever hold in his life. As they drove, the Ambassador felt great pity for the boy. The bravado was gone. In the face reflected in the rearview mirror, the Ambassador could see beads of sweat on the young man's forehead. Allah only knew how long the boy had lived in the United States, waiting for the moment he would be called upon to drive to his death. He remembered his own youth, the joy he had known in loving his wife and children, loving his work. What must it be like to waste a youth waiting for a single moment of glory, waiting to die?

The Ambassador would have felt a dark hopelessness as he looked at the young driver except for the dream he had had the night before. He only remembered bits and pieces. He remembered leaving his body and flying with creatures of light to join a great vortex. There had been work, he knew that, but he could not recall its structure or purpose. He only knew that it somehow gave him hope during the darkest moment of his life.

They slowed to approach the guard post outside the capitol building. The window beside the Ambassador opened, operated by the young driver from the main control on the armrest on the driver's door. The Ambassador recognized the young Marine Corporal who greeted him.

"Good morning, Ambassador Sassar," the Marine said. He simply waved at the documents the Ambassador held out to him. "That's all right, sir. I know you."

The electronic gates opened as the Marine looked to the front of the limo. "This isn't your usual driver, Ambassador," the Marine said, his hand now resting on the butt of the 9mm holstered on his hip.

"Stop him," the Ambassador pleaded, leaning out the window.

"Close the gates!" the Marine yelled as he drew the weapon, firing three quick shots toward the driver.

The heavy glass of the limo helped to deflect the bullets, protecting the driver just enough. The young fanatic floored the gas pedal, sending the limo crashing through the half-open gates.

"No!" the Ambassador screamed as the driver steered the limo not onto the driveway but across the sidewalk and onto the lawn, striving to get as close to the buildings as possible. Directly in the path of the limousine was a mother with two small children, one in a stroller and one holding her hand. The Ambassador scrambled forward, trying to reach the driver, trying to grab the wheel, but the design of the limo separated the driver and the passengers. The design intended for privacy blocked the Ambassador from any hope of reaching the driver.

That is when reality changed.

The limo did not strike the mother and children. It passed through them, or they through it. The Ambassador shook with an oddly pleasant sensation as, for an instant, the bodies of the mother and eldest child simply shared the same space that he occupied. In that moment, their feelings, their thoughts were his as well.

The car crashed into a decorative stone wall and stopped. The young man screamed, "Praise Allah," as he hit the radio control strapped to his chest that would detonate the bomb that was the car.

Nothing happened.

The young man sat there, stunned, hitting the button again and again. The Ambassador tried to open the door. It would not open. He realized that the terrorists had modified the handle so that it only opened from the outside. Amazed at himself, considering his age, he crawled through the still open window and ran back to the mother and two children. The young women stood, open-mouthed, staring at the limo. The baby was crying loudly, and the mother had taken the infant from the stroller and was holding it in her arms. The little boy was clutching his mother's leg, and she had a hand resting on the top of his head.

"Are you all right?" the Ambassador asked.

They looked into each other's eyes, and remembered the instant of total connectivity when their bodies had shared physical space. Without a doubt, the Ambassador knew he had a new daughter and two new grandchildren.

He looked around at the relative lack of destruction, and the Ambassador laughed in total joy. He lifted his face to heaven and spread his arms to the side. "In the hands of Allah," he yelled in Arabic.

That was when the Marines arrived, and he found himself facing the business end of several M-16s. He did as he was ordered and laid on the ground, his hands behind his back. As he felt the handcuffs going around his wrists, his mind touched on the uncertainty of his future. Diplomatic immunity should have been guaranteed, but it was uncertain times and international law was not as certain as it once was. At that moment, prison didn't sound like such an awful place.

Chapter Eight

The News

Kidwell's full cup of coffee grew cold on the table. It was totally forgotten. Anna's hair was disheveled, and her robe was tied awry, obviously done in haste. The two women stood with their houseguests, Aisha and Greg, in a semi-circle in front of the television. CNN blared the morning's amazing news from the Middle East and Washington.

They had all slept late after the mystical night they had shared as a part of the matrix. Kidwell was the first awake. She'd made coffee and taken her fresh cup to the couch where she'd turned on the television for the morning news, the volume softened so as not to disturb her housemates. Her quiet moment ended before she'd taken more than three sips from her coffee. Their mystical night was reflected in the morning's reality. The news told of failed weapons, of an aborted invasion codenamed Desert Lightning. *Desert Lightning had no power*, Kidwell thought. It told of a terrorist attack on the nation's capital that had ended in confusion but little destruction, an attack instigated by a fanatical young man codenamed the Scimitar. *The Scimitar has no edge*, Kidwell thought.

"Anna," Kidwell bellowed up the stairs. She knocked loudly on the guest bedroom door. "Wake up, everyone!" she called. "You've got to see the news."

The sleepy four stood as though transfixed in front of the television.

Anna turned to Kidwell, her very own military expert. "How can every weapon system fail for all the forces?" Anna asked.

"They can't," Kidwell answered.

"It did," Greg responded.

Kidwell laughed a choked laugh.

"What's so amusing?" Anna asked.

"I'll bet CentCom is really regretting pre-alerting the press pool about the pending invasion. I'll wager they wish they could have pretended this never happened."

"What does it all mean?" Aisha asked.

Greg smiled broadly, his uncombed hair standing at odd angles. "I'd say it means our night's work really did some good."

Anna's bedroom slippers shuffled across the floor as she made for the kitchen. "Before I can comprehend a miracle of this magnitude, I need tea."

"Me, too," Aisha said, following Anna to the kitchen.

"Coffee's made," Kidwell said to Greg. She picked up her own cup and took a sip. Her face curled in distaste as she realized the coffee was stone cold.

"I feel like I awoke to a whole new universe," Greg said.

"Perhaps we have," Kidwell responded. She heard the bang of pots and pans from the kitchen, and she knew Anna was gathering what she needed to make *migas*. It had been the plan for breakfast when they had all gone to bed, before they had even imagined what the night would hold.

"Watch the news for us, will you, Greg? We don't

want to miss anything. I'll bring you coffee, and we can all have breakfast in front of the TV."

Anna and Aisha were working in the kitchen. The two had become quite a culinary team since Aisha and Greg moved into the spare bedroom. Anna directed Aisha as they worked together to prepare ingredients for the *migas*. Kidwell and Greg had both gained a few pounds enjoying the products created by their life partners. The only drawback was the cumulative effect of spicy food – the chilies of Anna's native foods and the spices of Aisha's Middle Eastern dishes – were taking a toll on their genetically European stomachs. Last trip to the grocery store, Kidwell had invested in the industrial sized bottle of Maalox, and she and Greg happily passed the bottle after the evening meal. Kidwell poured fresh coffee for herself and filled a second cup for Greg. She returned to the living room, leaving the other two women talking excitedly as they worked. Half the time, Anna slipped unconsciously into Spanish and Aisha into Arabic, but both women seemed to understand the other. Kidwell's mind was too tired even to try to follow the conversation.

"Anything new?" Kidwell asked as she handed Greg his coffee.

"They interviewed some general in Iraq. He assured everyone that U.S. forces in the Middle East had the situation totally under control."

"Believe him?"

Greg laughed. "If that guy's the one who called the shots with what happened to us last night, we're all in a lot of trouble. Whoever's in control, it ain't him, thank God."

Kidwell smiled as she took a seat on the couch. "It's hard to know what to think or do."

                           Kayt C. Peck

"Sit and wait," Greg answered. A brief expression of envy flashed across his face. "You and Aisha seem to have a direct link to inside information."

"*Mí amora, ayudame,*" Kidwell heard Anna call from the kitchen. Kidwell jumped up to provide the help requested of her and arrived in the kitchen in time to be handed two plates full of the spicy egg mixture with freshly heated tortillas on the side. She carried the food into the living room with Anna and Aisha following behind, each carrying their own plates and steaming cups of tea.

The four companions sat before the television, laughing and talking, a sense of high festivity filling the room. The "special announcement" portion of the news did not last that long. No one had answers, and the press was at a loss whom to call upon as experts. They spoke with politicians and military advisors, diplomats and weapons experts. No one had an answer for the total, pervasive weapons failure that had left the militaries of the world, including terrorists, virtually impotent. By the time the four had finished their breakfast, the special news bulletins were gone, and the regular programming of a morning news/variety show was being broadcast. Of course, every guest spoke not of the movie, book, or recipe they were there to promote, but of the big news of the day. The author of a new novel gave the only believable explanation offered that morning.

"Seems like humanity has reached the point where we either destroy ourselves or save ourselves, with a little help from some outside force," the man said, slouched in the guest chair, glasses perched on his nose. He looked studiously prepared to appear just as an author should appear.

"May the Force be with you," the host quipped.

"God, I hope so," the author answered.

The laughter the host was inviting didn't come. Spontaneous applause from the studio audience that went on and on and on followed a rare moment of television silence.

"Wonder how many of them were in the matrix last night," Anna said.

"Bet the writer was," Greg responded.

"I've had enough of television. I'm going to check the Internet," Aisha said. She rose, taking her plate toward the kitchen before heading upstairs to borrow Kidwell's computer.

Kidwell gathered the other plates and cups and made for the kitchen. Greg and Anna maintained the television watch. Despite the enormity of the day's happenings, they drifted into a conversation about the author's last novel, a metaphysical action adventure set in Peru.

The phone rang just as Kidwell finished putting the plates in the sink, running water to soak the sticky egg residue.

"I'll get it," she called as she picked up the phone hanging on the wall in the kitchen.

"Brown-Montoya residence," she answered.

"Is this the famous Commander Brown?" a voice said.

Joy at the sound of a cherished voice mixed with the metallic taste of fear as Kidwell answered. "And this is the even more famous Admiral O'Hare," she responded.

"How are the mountains, Kidwell?"

"Still here and still beautiful. How's D.C.?"

"Still here, and, well, let's just say I envy you your

mountains."

"They're here waiting for you any time you and Sarah want to pay a visit."

"These old bones are getting a bit old for down-hill skiing."

Kidwell laughed. "These slightly younger bones still couldn't keep up with you when you were here last winter. Besides, there are quieter things to do in the mountains, you know."

"Sarah keeps bugging me about missing the Santa Fe Opera."

"You'll need to come in the summer for that. Now would work."

A long pause was Kidwell's initial answer. "Lord, doesn't that sound wonderful?" the Admiral answered, obvious longing in his voice. "How's Anna?"

"Still doing a fine job of keeping me in line."

"More than the Navy ever managed to do."

"She has a special talent for it," Kidwell responded. "So, how are things going in Washington really?"

The Admiral laughed. "Never dull, that's for sure." He laughed again, but it was strained. "If you ask me, it's time to go thirty degrees to starboard."

Kidwell forced herself to laugh. If either of their phones were tapped, it would be important that the conversation seem as casual as possible.

"Good memory, Admiral. You know, the offer's for real. Any time you need a vacation, our home is open to you."

"I know, and I can't tell you how comforted we are knowing that."

The visit continued. Kidwell asked about the Admiral's spin on the night's news, as much for the benefit of any potential eavesdropper as an effort to hear his input. He responded that he'd answer that question later, once he knew more of the facts. They talked about Tom Franconi and his pending knee surgery. They talked like the old friends they were. With every word, Kidwell wondered if it would be the last time she heard the voice of her friend and mentor. If she were in danger, his risk must be far greater.

Kidwell was still on the phone when she heard the television go off in the living room. She heard the agitated voices of her lover and their two friends. Anna stepped into the kitchen, her face pale and a piece of paper in her hand.

"Admiral, I need to go," Kidwell said. "We have company."

"Thanks for the visit, Commander."

"Any time," Kidwell answered as she put the receiver back in the cradle hanging from the wall. She turned to Anna. "What's wrong?"

Aisha and Greg followed Anna into the kitchen. They were also pale faced.

"Aisha got an email," Anna answered, handing Kidwell the paper.

The return email address was simply scimitar@ yahoo.com. The message included two sentences, two very frightening sentences.

"Death to the traitor. Death to the one who warned the infidels."

Kidwell looked up to her companions. "Looks to me like it's time to head for the mountains."

Chapter Nine

The Exodus

Kidwell and Hank Thomas leaned against the corral fence. Hank played with the ends of his handlebar mustache, keeping the points neat, no matter how disheveled the rest of his hair became where it was visible beneath his stained Stetson. They looked speculatively at the four horses and two mules tethered to the hitching rail beside the tack room. Three of the horses belonged to Kidwell and Anna. A fourth horse and the mules were on loan from the Tecolote Ranch, the massive outfit that Hank managed, in addition to his duties as local fire chief.

The closest mule eyed Kidwell with obvious skepticism. Kidwell returned the look.

"Never worked with mules before," Kidwell said.

"That's okay, Jody and Sam never worked with women before," Hank answered.

Kidwell looked sideways at her friend, her face expressing mild frustration. "That's certainly a comfort."

"Don't you worry none," Hank answered. "You just treat these mules the same way you treated the fellows in the fire department when you first moved here."

"Oh, Lord, does that mean there's going to be some head-butting?"

"Most likely, but nothing you can't handle."

Kidwell smiled as she remembered those early days when she and Anna were new volunteers with the fire department. There was a bad wildfire over the ridge from their house their first summer there. Kidwell decided that living in the forest was a lot like living aboard ship. Firefighting should be an all hands effort. There were already women on the fire department, wonderful women they learned to love and respect, but Kidwell was different. She came from the Navy with more firefighting training than most of the men, and with no hesitation to be among the first to face a fire – wildfire or structure. As she completed the required volunteer training, she learned quickly that shipboard firefighting had a lot in common with structure fires and almost nothing in common with wildland fires. To her own surprise, she found she enjoyed wildland firefighting immensely. All her life, she had known and loved the mountains on an equal footing with her love of the sea. She thought she had seen and appreciated the forest and plains in every condition possible. She had been wrong.

A forest fire had a sound, smell, and feel like no other. The first time Kidwell walked into a burn, she felt magic. It was a fire the way nature intended fire. Flames burned away undergrowth and the thick layer of duff (dead pine needles and leaves), barely touching or affecting the old growth of trees. On the one hand, Kidwell was amazed at the silence in the absence of all animal noise—no birds, no insects, no yip of a coyote or grunt of an elk. On the other hand, she was amazed at the music played by fire. The crackle and whine sounded like a hidden orchestra. She worked with other firefighters, not to face the fire head-on, but to pick the spot where they would allow it to go no further. Using hand tools, they created a scratch line in the duff. The sawyers followed, cutting away brush and trees to complete the firebreak. They watched the flames. At any point at which they thought the fire might grow in intensity and become a crown fire (moving into the canopy of the trees), they would fight it directly, using the hardy wildland trucks whenever possible, dealing out the meager water supply judiciously. Whenever needed, they fought directly, using hand tools or the weighty "piss packs" that were amazingly effective with their well-placed squirts of water. When they had finished the firebreak and the fire was under control, Kidwell was horrified the first time she saw the U.S. Forestry firefighters go back in and re-set the fire, burning out the undergrowth and duff within the entire contained area. It had taken time for her to understand that fire was a part of the natural cycle. Humanity's effectiveness at fire suppression created many of the conditions that exacerbated the natural lightning strike fires. Nature's small fires became huge terrors as they hit the heavy fuels created by human intervention. Those fires destroyed the forest rather than strengthening it.

Kidwell had not yet experienced any of the out-of-control crown fires, where fire leapt rapidly from tree to tree. She prayed she never did face a battle where the fire was winning. Those were the fires where survival was the primary mission of any firefighter. That is why each and every firefighter carried a square yellow or blue container on his or her belt during a wildland fire. They contained what was lovingly referred to in the field as the "kiss your ass goodbye" shelter. That was when the fire had outrun the firefighters, and there was no choice but to deploy the Jiffy-Pop shelters and wait to become popcorn. People had survived, but rarely unburned.

The most difficult training she had ever experienced, Navy or civilian, had been the session on surviving in the shelters. Panic was the worst enemy. The training film had interviewed a man who had survived with burns apparent on face and hands. He said he had stayed in the shelter for one reason and one reason only, to go home to his wife and children. Others had not. The training film played the audio from another fire, one where one of the firefighters within his shelter left his radio keyed. She listened to those who had, in panic, left their shelters and been sacrificed to the fire. The training ended with some of the psychological and meditative techniques that could help a firefighter fight the panic and survive. Kidwell had told Anna little about that training. She would have told her nothing, saving her the fear, if it had not been for the nightmares the following night. Anna had held her, asking about the dream.

"Fire," Kidwell had answered. "The fear isn't a bad thing, my love," she'd said. "It reminds me to respect the fire."

Anna held her closer. "*Querida,* must you really face the fires? There are others who—"

"I must," Kidwell answered. "Because I can."

Anna did not answer except to tighten her hold on her lover. She knew she would lose that debate.

As she stood beside Hank, Kidwell shook her head, dislodging the wave of memory and returning to the present.

"You'd best handle Sam and let Anna or Greg take Jody. Sam will be the one to put you to the test."

"Any suggestions?"

"Firm, but fair. Should come natural to you. Give a mule a little time to think things through. If it can be their idea as well as yours, it will go a lot easier."

Kidwell looked at the small bay gelding at the end of the line. "Aisha's only ridden a few times. You think the bay will be gentle enough for her?"

"He's one we let the owner's grandkids ride when they come to the ranch."

"Won't they miss him?"

"There are others. Besides," Hank paused to scrape mud from his boot onto the rail of the fence, "I forwarded your email about Desert Lightning to the owner. He called yesterday when he heard the news, all excited, wanting to know who you were and how you'd known."

Kidwell blushed, surprising herself. Hank's boss was a world-renowned actor who owned one of the state's largest ranches. She was embarrassed to know she had been a subject of discussion between the actor and Hank.

"What did you tell him?"

"I told him you were the most levelheaded metaphysical fruitcake I'd ever known."

Kidwell laughed. "Sounds like a good description to me."

The horses and mules were saddled and ready to go. Panniers on the mules were well filled with carefully thought-out survival supplies: tents, dried food, saws, axes, fishing gear, extensive first aid kit. The Tecolote Ranch farrier had worked most of the afternoon the day before and part of that morning, ensuring each animal's feet were trimmed and well shod. Kidwell's gear loaded in the pannier on one mule included a rudimentary farrier's kit. Their exile was likely to last longer than the shoes. Once these were worn thin and the hooves grew in need of trimming, the animals would have to go barefoot. Hopefully, by then, they would be hardened to the rocky slopes. Hoof trimming was a task where Kidwell's smaller hands were a major handicap. She was glad Greg would be along to help.

Hank was entrusting Kidwell with some of the ranch's precious animals, but Kidwell and Anna were entrusting him with a whole lot more.

"You got that power of attorney, Chief?" Kidwell asked.

Hank patted the pocket of his jean jacket. "Right here." Kidwell had asked him if he would be willing to handle their business after Master Chief Tom Franconi first delivered Admiral O'Hare's warning.

"You'll have to go by and sign the signature card on the joint account Anna and I set up with you on the account. The bank will automatically transfer my retirement check to that account, and I've put a good chunk of our savings in there as well. There should be enough to cover all the bills. Got the mailbox key?"

"Already put it on the ring with mine."

Kidwell sighed. She had done some frightening things in her time, but entrusting their home, their business, and much of their life to Hank was one of the most terrifying. It was not a fear that he would misuse the authority. She would not hesitate a moment to entrust Hank with her life, much less her money. It was an incredible feeling of vulnerability. Greg and Aisha made similar emergency plans before leaving Amber, leaving his sister as the trustee for their affairs. In the sleepless frenzy of preparation during the previous night, Kidwell and Greg had spoken briefly of the sensation of walking away from responsibilities.

"Everything 'bout ready?" Hank asked.

"Nearly. The others are in the house, gathering up personal items, still trying to decide what to take and what to leave, mostly things need to be left."

"Why aren't you in the house?"

"Already made my choices and they're packed in my saddlebags."

Hank nodded. He had seen first-hand Kidwell's ability to make command decisions under pressure. It was a different kind of fire, but he knew she faced fire. She would do what needed to be done.

The back door to the house opened, and Greg led Aisha and Anna down the path. Aisha walked with her arm looped through Anna's. Anna was shaking, tears threatening to form and fall from her eyes.

Kidwell met them on the path. She wrapped Anna in her arms.

"It will be all right, my love."

"But our home—"

"Will be all right. Hank will look after it. And if something happens, we'll simply rebuild when we get back."

"*Ah, Querida,*" Anna said into her lover's shoulder.

They kissed, deeply, something they had never done before in front of their friends and neighbors on the mountain. Neither noticed as Hank turned away, blushing.

The ranch foreman/fire chief cleared his throat and turned back to his friends. "Don't you worry about a thing, Anna. Everything will be just fine."

Kidwell stepped back. There was a change in her energy.

"Time to mount up and head for the hills."

Greg helped Aisha mount the quiet gelding before climbing onto his own horse. Kidwell untied Jody the mule and handed Anna the lead rope before she untied Sam and climbed aboard her grey Appaloosa.

"Got one more thing for you," Hank said.

"What's that?"

Hank walked to his truck and pulled a small electronic device from the console. He walked to Kidwell's horse, opened a saddlebag, and put the device inside.

"What's that?" Kidwell asked.

"The fire department's GPS so you can get your exact position via satellite. There's extra batteries, too."

"The department needs that."

"We'll get another."

The man walked to Kidwell and placed his hand on her knee from where he stood by her horse. "May it guide you to a safe place and bring you safely home again."

Kidwell nodded, blinking back tears. "Let's move out. The day's half gone, and we need to make some miles."

The lead rope was dallied around her saddle-horn, and when she urged her horse forward, the mule balked. Kidwell had no doubt who would win if it developed into a tug of war between her gelding and the mule. It wouldn't be the gelding. She tightened the lead-rope, nubbing the mule closer to the saddle, and she looked down at the wary, intelligent eyes of the long-eared animal. The others stopped, waiting for her.

"Sam," she said. "We've got adventure ahead of us, and I would really like for us to enjoy each other's company in the process." She waited a few moments, reaching down to rub around the animal's face. Abruptly, she urged her gelding into a tight circle, forcing the mule to follow or risk breaking his own neck. Two circles to the left, and one to the right, and then she leveled out into a straight line toward the trail ahead. The mule followed. So did the others.

Chapter Ten

The Haven

The horses and mules grazed on the lush grass of a high meadow, their saddles still in place but the cinches loosened. The bridles hung from the saddle-horns, and a long lead-rope staked or tied each horse to a tree. When the companions decided to take a long mid-day break, it had included extra grazing time for the animals.

Kidwell nabbed a large cottontail rabbit with the .22 rifle, and a rabbit stew, flavored with wild onion and sage they had gathered along the trail, was heating in a Dutch oven on the open fire. It would be a while before it was ready to eat. Both Kidwell and Greg were concerned that the rabbit be well cooked, eliminating the hazard of disease. It was only the fourth day into their exodus, and they had plenty of rations on the pack mules and saddlebags, but they were already doing well at living off the land. Greg was a godsend. His knowledge of edible and medicinal plants was already making a substantial difference in their diets. Since they would likely need the rations they carried to get them through the winter, living off the land was an important goal. Besides, fresh meat was a welcome treat, and Kidwell was using the relatively quiet firing of the .22 to train the animals for the sound of gunfire. When they found a long-term campground, they would be hunting for larger game, and she didn't want the blast of the 30-30 to be the first time the animals were exposed to the sound of a rifle.

Kidwell and Greg sat on a ground cloth beside the fire. Anna napped in the shade, and Aisha sketched a drawing of her gelding as he grazed. The GPS and a topographical map were spread on the ground cloth in front of Kidwell and Greg.

"Where to now?" Greg asked.

"We're well beyond familiar territory for me. Have been since the second day."

"I thought you and Anna backpacked or rode these mountains a lot."

"Maybe two or three trips a summer, usually just for three or four days. We know the area within a day's ride from our house very well, but that's it. Besides, I intentionally picked a route we had not taken before, just in case we're followed. Lots of folks know our favorite camping spots."

"You did well picking a path away from people. We haven't seen a soul for two days," Greg responded. He glanced at the Dutch oven. "Unless you count rabbits, snakes, and squirrels."

"Don't forget the bear," Kidwell said.

"I'd like to," Greg responded.

"Don't worry. A bear isn't likely to mess with a group this size, as long as we keep hanging our provision bags high and away from camp each night."

Greg smoothed the map that lay before him. "So, any high mountain valley with good water will do?"

"Just about, as long as it's relatively far from any community."

Greg looked at a larger map, one that gave less detail but showed all of northeastern New Mexico.

"Looks like we have some options."

"Yeah, unless there's a ski resort or a mine, there's not much reason for people to settle in the high valleys."

Aisha looked up from her drawing. "Ski resort, mine, or need to hide from lunatics in power."

Kidwell and Greg laughed. "Maybe we'll start a trend," Greg said.

"God, I hope not."

Aisha closed her sketchbook on the ground cloth and rose to her feet. "I'm going for a little walk."

"Don't go far," Greg said. "It could be easy to get lost up here."

She pointed to a nearby rock outcropping. "I'm just going up there. I'd like to draw this meadow from above. Maybe I can even include you two as you try to make sense out of squiggly green lines."

"They're mountains," Greg said.

Aisha looked down over his shoulder. "Looks like a bowl of spaghetti gone bad if you ask me."

"Let's hope we can find a good winter home somewhere in the spaghetti," Kidwell said.

Aisha laughed and began walking toward the woods.

"Call out if you need us," Greg said.

"I will."

The muscles in Aisha's thighs twinged as she walked. After four days, she was growing accustomed to the long hours in the saddle, but her body still protested. The second day had been the worst. She had tears in her eyes as she prepared to mount her gelding that morning. Greg had stepped away from his own horse and held her for a few moments, whispering encouraging words into her hair. He had helped lift her as she stepped into the stirrup and swung onto the horse. That little bit of help had made the pain in her legs and buttocks bearable as she mounted. They were all sore those first few days, but Aisha had moments of real agony.

Despite her pain, Aisha had grown to love the sure-footed bay gelding that had borne her faithfully and well. She groomed him every morning before saddling him. She had taken to grooming him every evening as well, just because she enjoyed the smell and feel of the huge, gentle animal. After four days, she was deeply regretting waiting so late in life to experience the joy of partnership between rider and horse.

Within twenty yards of entering the woods from the meadow, trees engulfed Aisha. She was glad she had taken her bearings before starting her walk. Still, she turned to her right, keeping the meadow in sight through the trees as she climbed toward the rock outcropping. At one point, Aisha looked to the ground as she placed a hand on a rock above her to steady her climb. There was a brief moment of disorientation as she felt the now familiar sensation of entering another reality. When she looked up, the pine trees were gone. In their place was a small stand of palm trees near the oasis she recognized from her first experience in the other realm. Seated beneath the trees was Khadija. Aisha smiled with joy. Whatever the message she was to receive, it meant she would have a few moments alone with the wife of the Prophet.

"Hello, daughter," the woman said. "How are your legs?"

"Sore."

"You should try riding a camel. After a day in the saddle, there's not a muscle that doesn't ache."

"I'll stick with horses. They smell better."

"And they don't spit."

Aisha walked to the woman. The spirit guide motioned for Aisha to take a seat on the carpet she had spread on the sand. Behind her was a small, traditional Bedouin tent.

Aisha sat, taking the earthen cup of fruit juice Khadija offered to her. As she drank deeply, she wondered if her body felt as refreshed by the drink as her spirit did.

"You have taken on a long and arduous journey," the spirit guide said.

"Yes, but you know about those."

"My husband and I know what it means to flee from the blade. The first time was terrifying. After that, I learned that we always found a better place."

"Will we?"

The spirit guide laughed. "That is why we are here, daughter, for me to tell you of that place."

Aisha leaned closer to her spirit guide. "Where?"

"Tell your ally to go to a place called Thunder Lake. She will know what I mean."

Aisha felt the disconcerting shift of changing reality. The last thing she heard was Khadija saying, "Take care, my daughter."

❧❧❧❧

Kidwell blinked in shock as Aisha told her about Thunder Lake.

"Thunder Lake? Are you sure?" Kidwell asked.

"Positive," Aisha answered.

Greg looked from Kidwell to Anna. Both faces expressed amazement.

"I take it you two know the place," Greg said.

"I know of it," Anna answered. "But I cherish my

life too much to actually go there."

"It doesn't matter. Whatever makes you fear the place, we must go there," Aisha said, a set expression around her mouth and eyes.

Kidwell placed her hand on Aisha's arm. "We will, my friend. Don't worry. We aren't foolish enough to ignore a spirit guide. Anna and I are just surprised."

"Why do you fear this place?" Greg asked.

"It's sacred ground to the Pueblo Indians. Rumor among those who enjoy the high country is that a non-Pueblo hiking Thunder Lake is likely not to make it back out again. That's if they ever find it."

"What do you mean?" Aisha asked.

"I was in college when I first learned of Thunder Lake. I saw it while looking at topographical maps in a mountaineering store in Taos. I asked about Thunder Lake, and the guy there told me not to go. He said he and a buddy decided to ignore the warnings and hike there once. They never arrived."

"But he came back alive."

"Not from Thunder Lake. I never was sure if it was a tall tale or not, but he had quite a story. He said he and his friend got within a half-day hike of the lake and then camped for the night. They awoke the next morning in an entirely different place, different mountain ranges, different trails. They could see a town in the valley below, so they broke camp and hiked down. They were in Colorado, near Durango, over two hundred miles from where they made camp the night before."

"Wow!" Greg said.

"And we will go there," Aisha said.

"*Sí, mija*. We will go there," Anna answered.

Kidwell and Greg turned to their maps and began plotting the new route.

Chapter Eleven

The Arrival

The mules and Kidwell's sure-footed Appaloosa had climbed the last hazardous high trail over the ridge as if it was a Sunday afternoon stroll. The rest of the horses and, most certainly the humans, had found the journey to be memorable, to say the least. Now the entire party rested on the other side of the ridge, thanking all the spirits that would listen for their safe passage. Aisha and her bay mount still shared the same wide-eyed expression. Kidwell was certain they never would have gotten the bay over the ridge if they hadn't tied his halter to the tail of Sam the mule. The bay had balked once, and the mule delivered one swift kick, making Aisha cry out in fear for her beloved mount. Fear of the mulish backside in front of him had distracted the sweet horse from fear of the steep trail, and the mule had steadied the horse when he started to stumble. Kidwell had been the only one to ride the route, secretly struggling to control her own fear. It was the only way she could lead both the mule and the bay. Aisha had walked the trail unencumbered by an animal, and Greg had led the other mule with his gelding tied to the tail of that animal, with Anna leading her own horse. The trail had been narrow with a terrifyingly steep drop-off to one side. For a time, Kidwell had regretted the decision to take the ridge instead of skirting around the mountain and approaching the valley to Thunder Lake from a less hazardous route. The path would have taken them directly through a Pueblo village – older than any European settlement in the United States – and she had not wished to risk a confrontation.

The switchback trail down the mountain to the high valley on the other side felt as safe and comfortable as a park sidewalk after their experience on the ridge. At a high meadow, they paused to catch their breath and steady their nerves. Greg fired the camp stove, and Anna collected the makings for a pot of chamomile tea. She had brought the tea as a sleep aid, but the mild sedative effect seemed a wise choice considering the state of their nerves. Aisha took a handful of the loose tea and fed it to her still frightened bay gelding. It seemed to help. Kidwell watched with interest and made mental note to add a bag of chamomile to their veterinary stores when they got home again. *Home again*...as she thought the phrase, she felt a tightness in her throat. After twenty years of traveling for the Navy, she had forgotten the pain of homesickness. In an odd way, it was nice to feel it again.

After deciding on a destination, the four had ridden hard for the past three days, not taking time to live off the land as they had during the earlier portion of the trip. Both Kidwell and Greg, the cautious ones of the group, were concerned about how much lighter the mules' packs were. Kidwell's supply of military surplus MREs (Meals Ready-to-Eat) had been their primary food for the rapid travel. In three days, they had consumed a tenth of what Kidwell had packed. Luckily, the high calorie content of the meals helped spread the supply. They had shared two MREs between the four of them each time they ate, keeping the candy bars, crackers, etc. for mid-day snacks. There had been times during the trip when Kidwell found herself looking longingly into the empty MRE bags, wishing for the small pack of cigarettes and matches that had been a part of military field rations for many decades. She had given up cigarettes over a decade before, but she still smoked a pipe occasionally. It was now more of a ceremonial practice than an addiction. Many people could not be as an occasional smoker, but Kidwell had never been a heavy smoker. Truth was she had taken up cigarettes in the Navy because, at some commands, smokers were the only ones who seemed to get a break.

Thunder Lake stretched below them as the four travelers looked down from their perch in the meadow. The blue of the water called a welcome, and Greg was pointing out the number of edible and medicinal plants that grew in the meadow. There should be plenty of game in the area surrounding the lake, and Kidwell was feeling more confident about finding sufficient food to survive the winter. Food would not be a problem, but another difficulty loomed. Far below, they could see a set of three teepees in the grassy plain beside the lake, and smoke puffed from a fire at the center of the circle of those teepees.

"So much for having the place to ourselves," Greg said.

"It will be fine. We're supposed to be here," Aisha said.

"I hope you're right," Kidwell responded.

Anna lovingly hit her lover on the shoulder. "*Querida*, you worry too much."

For the moment, there was nothing they could

do about the people at the lake, so they settled down to more immediate needs—food and rest. The animals munched happily on the rich grass as the humans heated their MREs using the hydrogen chemical reaction included in the MRE container. Aisha remained amazed every time she saw them use cold water to create heat. She asked how it worked, and Kidwell was surprised to realize that she didn't have a clue. She had used MREs for years and never before wondered. Despite the lack of understanding, she was grateful for the warm food as she and Anna split a beef stew from a bag, each taking a portion in their blue enamel camp plates.

They finished their meal and cleaned their plates using leaves and grass to remove the majority of the food, finishing with a light rinse from their drinking water. They'd wash later, when a ready supply of water was available. They were packing away plates and trash when a group of five riders came out of the trees from the trail below. Kidwell's hand went automatically to the pistol strapped to her side, and she considered pulling her rifle from the scabbard on her saddle. She looked at the dark-haired horsemen below and saw no sign of a weapon. Anna took the lead, walking away from the others and down the trail toward the riders. She stopped about ten yards down the trail, and Kidwell trotted to take a place beside her lover. The intensity of the protectiveness she felt surprised her.

As they watched the approaching party, one rider broke free from the others and loped his horse toward them, waving as he rode. The flowing black hair of the young man danced in the breeze, adding to the beauty and motion of the loping horse. A broad smile showed flashing white teeth as he pulled his black and white paint horse to a stop a few feet from Anna and Kidwell.

"Where have you been? We've been waiting for you," the young man said.

⚛︎⚛︎⚛︎⚛︎

The four travelers sat in the council circle, nestled in the shade of massive Ponderosa pines that grew near the edge of the lake. Like a few of the Pueblo tribes-people in the circle, the four companions rested on woven blankets—the two-for-ten-dollar variety made in Mexico and sold at truck stops throughout the Southwest. Most of those present sat on folding lawn or camp chairs, just as the Native Americans had at the many public powwows that Kidwell and Anna had attended. The women had learned early that the rule at powwows was BYOC: bring your own chair. Kidwell wondered how the chairs had gotten there. Most present had arrived by foot or horseback, although she had noticed a couple of wagons parked at the edge of the campsite. She suspected that a few chairs came each trip and stayed in one of the permanent lodges. There was one adobe structure and another, more recently built, where the Pueblo had borrowed from the tradition of the Navajo – or Diné as they were known in their own tongue – in building a log, eight-sided hogan.

All of the northern Pueblos and most of the southern were represented around the circle. No one, no person that is, had called the gathering. At each Pueblo, at least one, and sometimes more of the shamans or respected elders, had received a dream or vision telling them to go to Thunder Lake to await four messengers, including the one who would be champion for the people. The Pueblos reference to a champion troubled Kidwell. It hinted at a battle to come. She mentioned her concern to Anna, and her lover had shaken her lovingly.

"*Mi amora*, haven't you learned yet to take things one at a time?" Anna asked.

Not all of the Pueblos had listened. Kidwell overheard two of the elders speaking about one tribal group to the south. No one had arrived from that reservation.

"Aye, no," one elder said. "It started with the damned Interstate crossing their reservation, and now the casinos. It's made them forget what it means to be Indian."

Nor was the gathering just of Pueblos. Martin Gonzales, the young man who had first greeted them and had appointed himself as their official guide, was a Jicarilla Apache who had been living amongst the Navajo near Crownpoint in western New Mexico. He was an exception to the calling of the Pueblos. Martin's summons had been an individual one. Despite his amazing capacity for energetic optimism, there was a serious young man hiding behind his smiling face. He had traveled initially to the Navajo, cousins to the Apache, seeking new teachers as he continued down his spiritual path. He made a living in construction, working where he could at jobs in western New Mexico, but it was the ceremonies, the vision quests, the sage, cedar, and the tobacco that ruled his life. The young man had been an eager part of the matrix to stop the war of all wars, but he had continued to feel troubled, certain there was more to be done. Many times, the construction jobs that supported him kept him working until after dark, but he tried to make it home by sunset every day. He lived a humble life in a shack he had borrowed on Navajo tribal land, but his flute, medicine pouch, and pipe all held a place of honor in his home. The young man would walk to a ridge near his home each day at sunset, scatter corn pollen to the six directions, and flute to the setting sun, praying in the way Indians seem to know best—listening rather than speaking.

One evening, Grandmother Spider herself came to Martin. He had known visions before, but none that walked within his waking world. Martin cried with joy at her presence and listened with all his heart to her instructions to go to Taos Pueblo, where he would join the people there in a journey to Thunder Lake. There they would await four messengers, including a champion, a champion who would guide him in the way of the peaceful warrior. He was to serve and guard the four messengers, freeing them for their mission.

The four visitors watched as Henry Shendo, the elder at the head of the circle, took the pipe from the fire-keeper. When the pipe had finished its journey around the circle, the fire-keeper had puffed deeply, finishing with reverence the sacred tobacco left in the pipe after all had smoked. Kidwell had wished she could take time to study the pipe when her turn had come. It was not like the wooden-stemmed pipe she had always seen and used, including the pipe that lay on the mantel at home, a gift from one of their Cherokee friends. This pipe was a simple one, made entirely of clay. She remembered seeing a mold of a similar pipe that archeologists at an Anastasi site in Arizona had found. Kidwell remained silent, as she took smoke, and smudged herself with the puffs of tobacco smoke from the bowl of the pipe before passing it on to Anna on her left.

The elder spoke, with no need to raise his hand or in any way draw attention to him. The group was silent, reverent within the ceremony. Few Anglo groups could have sat silent and still for the length of time it took for the pipe to pass to all in the circle. Peaceful patience was a forgotten skill in American mainstream culture.

"We have all been called here to welcome our honored guests," Henry said, motioning with his chin toward the four travelers. "I believe all here joined in the spirit struggle that stopped the power of Desert Lightning and the Scimitar. We know that great things are happening and that these four have a special role to play." Henry paused, taking time to gaze into the eyes of Kidwell, Anna, Aisha, and Greg. "We do not know what will come next, and neither do you. We must be on constant watch and listen with our hearts and souls for the guidance of the spirits." He leaned toward the four, and there was a feeling that he had crossed the space between them. From twenty-feet away, Kidwell felt the intensity of his presence. "Listen with discernment. Not everything from the spirit world serves the balance of the universe." He leaned back and, once again, looked more like a tired old man who didn't like sleeping on the ground. "There is shelter here, and you four are welcome to use it. We shall leave the traveling lodges here, and the structures the Taos people have built here are open to you as your homes for the time you must be here. We have brought food and medicinal plants to see you through the winter, and we have gathered wood so that you will have fuel to keep you warm. There is grain for your animals for the coldest, snow-covered months."

He paused, looking toward the four.

Kidwell looked to her companions, and realized they were looking to her, waiting for her to serve as spokesperson.

"Your gifts are more than we could have dreamed," Kidwell said. "We had dreaded a long cold winter, with little time to prepare for it. Thank you for all you have done. We shall strive to be worthy of these gifts." Kidwell looked at Anna and smiled softly. "As my partner is fond of reminding me, I should have known that what we needed would be provided."

Henry smiled softly before continuing the ceremony. Shamans from the different Pueblos, each in their native tongue, said prayers. Aisha surprised all present when she took a turn, praying in Arabic. Despite the atmosphere of reverence, as time passed, there was a hint of impatience in the air. Once they left the circle, food awaited. The four travelers had left a brace of rabbits, smothered in wild onions and sage, slow cooking in the Dutch oven over the coals of their campfire. All present had a contribution waiting for the feast to come. Kidwell and Anna anticipated the Indian tacos and fry bread that they knew awaited. Hunger has a way of distracting even the most devout.

❧❧❧❧

Three different "drums," teams of drummers and singers, took their turns at the ceremonial drum at the edge of the fire circle. The sharing prevented any "drum" from becoming exhausted and allowed each team an opportunity to join in the dancing and help themselves to the feast. It was Aisha's first Native American ceremony, and she watched in fascination.

There is no way to describe the sensation when even the hearts of those listening seemed to beat in sync with the throbbing of the drum. There is something massive about the oneness that develops as the drummers and singers play the traditional song and the dancers put the sound to motion. All four joined in the friendship dance, pulled into the circle by the headman and headwoman, and now they sat on their woven ground cloths, watching from just outside the ceremonial circle.

Kidwell leaned forward as she realized what was coming next, a Gourd Dance honoring veterans. She attended many Gourd Dances, and she had always longed to join the circle, dancing the simple but intense movements of the dance. She had never felt comfortable enough to ask to join. Kidwell felt a twinge of mild envy as she watched the veterans don their red and blue sashes, pick up their fans and their gourd rattles to take their place in the circle. Right behind them danced another circle, the family and friends who wished to honor them. Kidwell turned from the dance when she felt a hand on her shoulder. Martin knelt beside her, holding a folded bundle tied loosely with leather thongs.

"I brought something for you," said the smiling young man.

"Thank you, Martin. What is it?" Kidwell asked.

There was pain in his eyes, shining past the smile on his face. "These were my father's," he said.

Martin laid the cloth on the blanket beside Kidwell. As he did, Kidwell saw the blue and red of a veteran's sash, along with a rattle, fan, and the bone bandolier that some dancers wore. On the sash, Kidwell recognized the insignia for Army Rangers.

The ribbons were ample in number and impressive in their meaning—the Purple Heart, holding one star for a second award, and the Bronze Star were among them. She saw the distinctive color of a Vietnam service ribbon.

"Martin," she said in shock. "You aren't giving me these, are you?"

"Just a loan, until you can make your own," he answered. "He would want you to use them today."

"Is your father…?"

"He died four years ago. The Agent Orange finally got him."

"I'm so sorry."

The young man smiled sadly. "I'm not. He lived an honorable life. I'm proud to be his son."

Kidwell put her hand on the young man's forearm. "And he must be proud that you are his son."

A troubled expression creased Martin's brow. "I hope so. At my age, I wonder if he would wish that I could wear them myself."

"You've considered joining the service?"

"Who can truly be a man until he's proven he can be a warrior?" Martin asked.

Kidwell glanced back at the dance, searching for inspiration. "Martin, the best warriors are those who seek peace."

"My father said something similar. Sometimes he regretted his service in Vietnam."

"Many did, but how, specifically, did it affect your father?"

"He said that being a warrior means nothing unless battles are fought with honor."

"Did he feel that war was without honor?"

"Sometimes he wondered. That's what kept me

from joining when I turned eighteen."

"How so?"

Martin looked to the sky. "I sought guidance from the spirits, and I looked at the battles our country sought."

"And?"

"The honor was not strong and clear. I held back."

Kidwell turned fully to the young man. "I'm glad, Martin. If you hadn't, I would not have such a brave young man ready to fight beside me now."

Martin blushed. "I am ready to learn from you."

Kidwell laughed. "And I from you."

Kidwell donned the sash and the bandolier. She picked up the gourd and the fan, and she took her place in the circle of veterans. The rhythm of the dance ran through her until she was lost in the sound and the motion. She felt the presence of others behind her, dancing in the place for those who wished to honor her service. She glanced over her shoulder. Anna was there and so was Martin.

As she danced, Kidwell wept.

Chapter Twelve

The Mountain

The smell of wood smoke hung inside the lodge like incense. It was a pleasant sensation as Kidwell gradually drifted from sleep to the waking world. There was a slight chill in the air beyond the blankets that covered her and Anna, making Kidwell snuggle even closer to her lover's back, burying her face in the familiar softness of Anna's long, black hair.

In that moment, happiness lived. It was a presence in the lodge, living and breathing with a distinctive personality Kidwell would always know and love. Happiness lived, as pure and real as painfully cold spring water or the mixed colors of a sunset peeking beyond the mountains.

If this is what it means to be in exile, bring it on, Kidwell thought, the last of sleep drifting from her mind. The happiness lived, even as the ache of her bladder made her realize she had to leave the cocoon of the bed she shared with Anna. That bed was amazingly comfortable. The Pueblos who had erected the lodge had dug a shallow pit underneath the bed, leaving loose dirt at the bottom. Fragrant pine needles, covered with soft blankets, filled the pit. It was a human nest, pure and simple, and neither Kidwell nor Anna had known a more comfortable bed.

Kidwell eased out of the covers, careful to

keep the cold air away from the sleeping Anna. The flap of the teepee Kidwell and Anna had adopted as home did its job well. When Kidwell pushed the canvas (modern day substitute for the buffalo hide of old), she felt the damp chill of the morning. At this altitude, the mornings could be painfully cold, even in the summer. Besides, summer was ending. The day before, as Kidwell and her lover gathered mushrooms in the woods, Anna pointed out the hint of color in the leaves of the aspen. Fall would come two to three weeks earlier for the four in their haven than it would for those living in the lowlands. Thanks to the help of their Pueblo hosts, they were ready for winter with food and wood stockpiled for the long, snowy months.

After a quick detour to the latrine they had dug in the woods near their campsite, Kidwell made her way to the adobe structure that the companions now used as the common room. It was there that they cooked and socialized. The permanent party was now five instead of four, with Martin making a welcome addition to the group. His knowledge of medicinal plants exceeded Greg's, largely due to what he had gleaned from both Apache and Navajo healers. Besides, Martin's ready smile and quick wit added a dimension of laughter that improved their existence like a jar of honey in the pantry of life.

When Kidwell entered the adobe, she found Aisha already there, sitting in a folding chair beside the wood stove she had already fired. Aisha sat with an enameled metal cup filled with the strong, black tea that was her preferred morning drink.

"Morning," Kidwell said. "Greg still asleep?"

"Didn't you hear his snores on the walk over here?"

Kidwell laughed. "No, can't say that I did. Are they pretty impressive? I didn't notice them when we were traveling."

Aisha smiled. "Not really. Don't tell him. I find them comforting, but I don't want to give up my right to tease him."

Kidwell went to the shelves at the back of the main room. She filled a coffee pot from the five-gallon collapsible jug they used as their ready water supply and then dumped three scoops of coffee grounds directly into the water. Both Aisha and Anna preferred tea, but Kidwell and Greg had become accustomed to the strong, black "cowboy coffee." A half-cup of cold water into the pot just before pouring sent most of the grounds to the bottom, leaving a strong liquid that was even better with a spoonful of raw sugar.

Aisha's portable easel leaned against her chair. When they had been choosing the essentials for the trip, no one had debated the easel with the wooden box in the base that held paints and brushes. The companions knew that Aisha's art would prove important. Aisha had almost decided to leave behind her preferred medium, acrylics, because she knew she would be unable to take canvases with her. Watercolor paper was much less bulky. Luckily, she had not. The watercolor paper was almost gone, but the acrylics proved perfect for the wealth of natural canvas – wood, bone, stones – Aisha now gathered in the woods. She even had a few canvases now. The Taos Pueblo sent someone with supplies and news at least once each week. Hesitantly, Aisha had asked about canvas. The next week, two packages of the simple board canvases were among the supplies, along with a fresh supply of acrylic paint.

"Ready for breakfast?" Kidwell asked.

"Yes, sounds good," Aisha answered.

Kidwell reached inside a worn and folded paper bag and retrieved four biscuits they had cooked the day before in the small oven in the wood stove. She placed the biscuits on a camp plate and took a butter knife and a jar of honey from the shelves. Aisha moved her chair to the table near the adobe's only glass-filled window, and Kidwell took a seat at the table as well. Wooden shutters covered the other windows. Later that day, when the sun had warmed the air, they would open those shutters, but for now, that one window offered the only light. Kidwell wondered at the luck and determination of those who had dared bring window-glass up the rough trail.

"I was going to go look for lamb's quarter this morning," Kidwell said. "Maybe we can start out together."

"Sounds good, both the starting together and the lamb's quarter. Fresh greens for lunch would be wonderful," Aisha answered.

After they finished breakfast, they wrote a note in charcoal on the flat piece of wood that now hung by the door. Notes were short and simple but could be critical if one of them failed to return from an excursion. This day, Kidwell's said, "Gathering plants. Meadow, NW (northwest)," while Aisha's said, "Painting. Ridge, N (north)." The system worked. When they returned, they simply washed the charcoal from the wood, and it was ready to use again.

The note board was just a part of the routine that had developed since the four had arrived at the haven. It varied somewhat. They had grown to accept the steady trickle of pilgrims that began arriving at their lakeside home since their first week living in the lodges. Some were Indian. Some were White. Some arrived speaking in broken English from lands far away. Aisha's knowledge of Arabic had proven particularly important. Every party arrived with a Taos guide. Each of the pilgrims shared one thing in common; they came because a vision or a dream had directed them to the Taos Pueblo. The people of Taos were serving as gatekeepers for what was happening beside Thunder Lake.

When the pilgrims arrived, they listened to the stories of the companions, and they made their own solitary journeys into the woods. Almost without exception, all the pilgrims returned with stories of visions of their own. Aisha and Kidwell remained the pivot point of the guidance and revelations. They had each received instruction to record their experiences and their thoughts, and the weekly supplies provided by the Taos now included a constant supply of lined writing pads and cheap pens and pencils. As Kidwell and Aisha filled those pads, they returned them to the Taos emissaries for safekeeping.

Some days, they simply enjoyed life in the mountains. As Kidwell and Aisha walked in companionable silence, they hoped today would be such a day. Kidwell carried a canvas bag slung over her shoulder and Aisha walked with easel in hand. It was a good day to enjoy some of the last of the summer sun. When they reached the point where their paths and morning missions diverged, smiles and brief waves were their only expression of goodbye.

Kidwell walked through a sparse stand of Ponderosa pines, toward a meadow not far from the camp. Aisha had barely disappeared from sight when

Kidwell felt the now familiar feeling of soul leaving body. The sensation made her smile, a smile that remained on her physical form as it crumpled to the ground. Kidwell hovered above, looking around for White Buffalo Calf Woman. Instead, she saw a white form, glowing with such intensity that her physical eyes could not have looked upon it. The light was more than light. She felt it with senses she did not know she had. It was beyond wonderful. Beauty had been distilled and handed to her for a moment of intense pleasure. Power emanated from the being as well, triggering for Kidwell a wonderful fear. There was nothing human about the creature, and she felt certain it had never known the simple realities of a physical self.

"Who are you?" she thought to the being.

"A teacher for the warrior," the being thought back. If she'd had her physical self, she would have wept with joy at the pleasure of the being's thoughts touching her.

"Are you…are you an angel?"

"I serve the Universe as best I can." It was all the answer she would get.

"Who is the warrior?"

The next thought was a whiff of amusement. "Do you not know?"

Kidwell felt disappointment. She had hoped to avoid this task. "Yes, I know."

"I have something for you, to help you serve the Universe." Out of the glow reached a hand, and in that hand was the most beautiful sword Kidwell had ever seen. She knew the being wished her to take it, but in that moment, touching the object required more courage than she could muster.

"Please, take it," the being said telepathically.

Drawing from strength outside herself, Kidwell reached toward the sword. As soon as she took the object from the being, the object changed form, altering from a blade of light and a hilt covered in jewels from the sun, to a simple steel sword, not even elaborate or royal in appearance. A simple Celtic knot made of forged metal topped the hilt. Somehow, it looked and felt familiar in Kidwell's hand.

"I don't know how to use a sword," Kidwell thought.

"Yes, you do."

At his words, Kidwell looked down at her own hand. A beefy fist replaced her petite fingers, which led upward into an arm covered in a rug of reddish hair. Then she remembered. No, she did not remember. He remembered.

Kidwell threw back his head and laughed, laughed with the sheer joy of remembering all he had been in that life. A full, red-beard covered his face, and a great kilt covered his lower body. The giant of a warrior remembered the battles, remembered the loves, seeing Anna as she had been in that life, the priestess he protected and served. He raised the sword and made it dance in the air, practicing the familiar moves that had made him one of the greatest warriors of his clan.

Then Kidwell was back, the diminutive warrior of modern times who fought with her mind more than her body. In both lives, she had known how to use the weapons of war but only in service to peace.

"The sword will be there when you need it, and so will the memories of how to use it."

The being was gone, and Kidwell rose from the dirt of the trail, still filled with the joy and pain of the remembered life. She would gather the lamb's quarter before returning to camp to tell her story. She needed the time to savor the experience just for herself.

⁂

When Aisha felt the familiar sensation of soul leaving body, she set her easel on the ground and kept moving, or at least her spirit did. She did not bother to look back at her physical self when she felt the sensation change from walking to floating. She simply looked forward to another visit with Khadija as she moved toward the now familiar oasis in the desert.

"Hello, daughter," Khadija called.

"Hello, Mother," Aisha answered.

The spirit guide had a cup filled with juice and was holding it toward Aisha as Aisha reached the palm tree and took a seat on the ground cloth.

"It is good to see you again," Aisha said.

"I watch you always, my daughter."

Aisha blushed with pleasure at that thought. "Do you have a message for me today?"

"A gift," Khadija said. She reached beside her and retrieved an elaborately embroidered bag covered in symbols and Arabic words, only a fraction of which Aisha understood. The spirit guide pulled back the flap and exposed a waterproof lining, probably a sheep's bladder. A sweet and pleasing smell came from the salve held inside the bladder.

"What is that?" Aisha asked.

"A salve that will heal what your human medicine will not," Khadija answered.

"I will carry it with honor."

"No need. It will simply be there, ready in hand, when the time comes for you to use it."

And that was the end of business. They talked,

simply talked, visiting about womanly things. Each woman sharing the pain and joys they had known, the challenges and gifts of the men they loved. They talked. It was one of the most magical moments Aisha had ever known. She did not realize the moment when the vision transformed into a dream until her eyes opened, and she found herself lying on her side in the pine needles. She lay there for some moments, savoring the memory.

When Aisha arose, she decided to postpone her painting. She wanted to return to the lodge she and Greg shared to sleep, hoping to retrieve the moment in her dreams. Aisha started back down the return path, meeting up with Kidwell at almost the same point where they parted company. They each looked at the glow in the other's face.

"So, you had another experience, too," Aisha said.

"Yes, and you?"

"Of course."

"Did they give you another message?" Kidwell asked.

"No, a gift," Aisha responded.

"Me, too."

They turned together to walk the path to their temporary home, eager to share their stories not only with each other but also with their mates and Martin. They were only a quarter mile from camp when they rounded a corner of a trail to find a man waiting for them. Both women stared at the figure, amazed and confused. He wore a full, black beard, flecked with grey, and his only clothing was a full-length garment made of rough cloth and tied with a sash made of the same cloth. Sandals were his only foot protection on the rough trail. When they two women stopped, he walked toward them.

"Hello," he said in a tongue neither woman knew yet somehow understood.

"Hello," Kidwell answered. "Can we help you?"

The man laughed. "You already have—me and many others," he answered, still speaking in the strange tongue they miraculously understood.

"Who are you?" Aisha asked.

"My name is Peter."

Kidwell and Aisha looked at each other and then at the ground around them, expecting to see their physical selves lying atop the floor of pine needles. The man laughed again, a huge laugh that exuded a contagious amusement.

"I asked to visit you instead of having you come to me," the man said. He looked through the trees and toward the lake beside their camp. "I wanted to smell these mountains and especially see the water, and perhaps fish a bit. What is that vessel you've been using?"

"A canoe," Kidwell answered.

"When we get to your camp, might we…?"

"It would be a great honor to share a canoe with you."

The man smiled. "I am a simple fisherman."

Kidwell shook her head, not knowing how to respond to a statement so true and yet so inadequate. The man turned and led the way back to the camp.

Greg, Anna, and Martin were sitting in the sunlight in front of the common house when they saw the three approaching. They walked to meet them, curious about the man.

"Greg, Anna, Martin, meet Peter," Aisha said as

they stood together.

"Hello, Peter," Greg said.

"*Beinvenidos*," Anna said.

"Welcome to the party," Martin said.

"I am glad to be here," Peter answered in the language none of them knew but they all understood. While he spoke, his eyes were focused on the water of the nearby lake.

Greg, Anna, and Martin stood wide-mouthed and confused.

"Uh, where are you from, Peter?" Greg asked.

"Greg, he's, well, he's *the* Peter," Kidwell said.

Both Greg and Anna looked to the ground, assuming they would see their physical forms. Martin just looked confused.

"He came to see us, instead of having us come to him," Aisha said.

Greg, Anna, and Martin looked at each other.

"Cool," Martin said.

"Why?" asked Greg.

"Is that the canoe?" Peter asked, pointing to the vessel beached nearby.

"Yes," Kidwell answered. She lifted the canvas bag filled with lamb's quarter from her shoulders and handed it to Anna.

"Sorry to desert you guys, but we have some fishing to do."

Kidwell walked into the common house and returned with two rods and a small, plastic tackle box. Peter followed as she made her way to the canoe. They pushed-off with ease, Peter automatically taking the place in the stern, piloting the canoe as though he had done it all his life...lives.

Fish surrounded the canoe like rats coming to the

Pied Piper. Kidwell's line had fallen into the water as they paddled from the shore. The rod jerked and danced, and Kidwell pulled in the largest trout she had ever caught as it hung from the bait-less hook. Peter didn't cast his line. He simply dipped a hand into the water and pulled a fish to him. He held the creature gently, lovingly.

"You have a beautiful place for fishing," the apostle said.

"It's usually more of a challenge," Kidwell said.

He laughed. "It is enough for me to enjoy the feel of a boat beneath me and the smell and feel of the water and the air."

They had paddled into the middle of the small lake and now drifted freely. Carefully, Kidwell straddled the front bench seat and turned to face her companion.

"Why are you here, Peter?"

"To give you what you need."

"What we need to do what?"

"To bring back the true message." The apostle leaned forward, a book now in his hand. "This will help."

Kidwell read the title on the cover, *The Nag Hammadi Library*. "I know about this. It's the Gnostic Gospels," she said. "I have a copy in my library at home."

She took the book from Peter, noting first the woven pastel bookmark like the one she had at home. Next, she realized one corner of the cover was bent, and when she opened the front cover, she saw a very familiar bookplate proclaiming ownership.

"This is the copy from my library at home," she said.

The man's beard moved noticeably from the enthusiasm of his smile. "There is a new passage marked for you."

Kidwell noticed a piece of parchment nearly three-quarters of the way through the tome. She turned to the *Apocalypse of Peter* and read the marked passage:

They will cleave to the name of a dead man, thinking that they will become pure. But they will become greatly defiled and they will fall into the name of error and into the hand of an evil, cunning man and a manifold dogma, and they will be ruled heretically. For some of them will blaspheme the truth and proclaim evil teaching. And they will say evil things against each other (there was a skip in the marking) *…But many others, who oppose the truth and are the messengers of error, will set up their error and their law against these pure thoughts of mine, as looking out from one perspective, thinking that good and evil are from one* (source). *They do business in my word* (again, a skip) *… And there shall be others of those who are outside of our number who name themselves bishop and also deacons, as if they have received their authority from God. They bend themselves under the judgment of the leaders. These people are dry canals.*

"I remember clearly the day the Savior said those words. On that day, the priests praised him, but he seemed not to notice. He spoke with me alone of a future so distant I could not imagine its existence. He told me to hold those words for a time when they would be needed," Peter said. "I passed them on only to the followers I trusted most."

"And when the time came, they buried them for seventeen centuries," Kidwell responded.

"Yes."

Kidwell looked down at the passage. "Who was he talking about?"

"Do you not know?"

Kidwell looked out over the water. She thought of the hate she had seen, of what had happened to so many formalized religions.

"Yes, I know," she answered.

"It is time to reclaim what the Savior began."

"Are people ready?"

"Some, perhaps even enough."

Kidwell looked toward the distant shore. Her companions were sitting outside the common house, watching the canoe from a distance. "Why us?" she asked.

"Because you listened. Because you were chosen."

Kidwell nodded her head. She suspected it would be her only answer.

Peter reached into the water and gently captured another fish. He caressed the creature for a moment before releasing it back into the water and then picked up his paddle. Kidwell started to turn, retrieving her own paddle from where she had it leaned against the side.

"I can manage this craft," Peter said.

Kidwell remained sideways on the seat as the big man dipped his paddle in the water. Within moments, they were zipping across the surface, and Peter had a broad smile as he returned them to the shore beside the common house by a very indirect route.

Aisha, Anna, Greg, and Martin were waiting for them when they beached the canoe. Greg and Martin grasped the bow, and pulled the craft onto dry ground with Kidwell and Peter still seated. They both stepped out of the canoe as the others gathered around them.

"Will you join us for lunch?" Anna asked Peter.

Peter sighed. "My job is done now. I must return."

Kidwell held the book up for the others to see. "We have a new task."

"What is it?" Aisha asked.

"To return the work of Jesus to its intended path," Peter answered.

Greg whistled in astonishment. "That will be no small task."

Peter placed his hand on Greg's shoulder. "You will never be alone."

"For Christians or for Muslims?" Aisha asked.

"I pray there will come a time when there is no need for that distinction," Peter said.

Kidwell thumbed through *The Nag Hammadi Library*. "But so much was lost during the centuries these works were buried."

"Perhaps not," Peter said as he waved his hand.

"What do you mean?" Martin asked.

Peter led the way as he walked to the common house. He opened the door and held it wide for the others to enter. Standing in the middle of the room was an earthen jar, tightly sealed with a material none of the companions had seen before.

"Here they are, just as they were the day they were buried," Peter said.

The companions made a semi-circle around the jar, eyes wide with a shared sense of awe.

"What do we do with it?" Anna asked.

There was no answer. They turned as a group to the doorway. Peter was gone.

They turned back to the jar.

"We do what we've always done," Kidwell said. "The best we can."

Chapter Thirteen

The Darkness

The *brujo* spoke dark words, words taught to him by a Master few humans would admit existed. He spoke dark words and dropped human hairs into a small fire in a caldron before him. As the hairs withered and evaporated into foul smelling smoke, a woman died in a hospital four hundred miles away.

He would have preferred to have taken his time, caused the woman great anguish as she died of the cancer that consumed her body, but that is not what he had been paid to do. The woman's son had come to him not out of hate, but out of mercy. The son could no longer bear to watch her suffering and had not the courage to end it with his own hand. The *brujo* would have made the death painful for his own pleasure, but he needed the handful of dollars and the occasional *pesos* that came to him from those who gathered their courage to approach the Dark One in his desert cave and pay him to work his magic. Many came with a misguided notion of the good he could bring to their lives, and he let them keep their illusions as long as they let him keep their money. The money fed his belly and gave him the few worldly goods he desired. One would be tempted to say worldly pleasures, but this would have been incorrect. The Dark One had long forgotten what it meant to enjoy a simple pleasure.

Hate sustained him. It had sustained him for over two centuries, ever since the Master had granted him immortality in exchange for unquestioning servitude. There had been a reason he had agreed at the time, but the *brujo* no longer remembered the reason. Nor did he remember the initial cause of his hate. Hate was enough. It sustained him, and he took every opportunity to savor its power.

Once, he had been a man. Deep within the recesses of his soul, there was even a hint of the flavor of love he had known before the hate became bigger. Once, he had a name. It was gone, even in his memory. The indigenous people that lived near his mountain simply called him the Dark One, despite the flashing blue of his eyes. In all other ways, his appearance was of the dark-haired, dark-skinned tribes of the pre-white occupation. The eyes were just another mystery in the past he no longer remembered.

He felt the Master behind him, and the metallic taste of fear filled his senses. Never once, never in two centuries, had he failed to know that taste when in the presence of his Master.

"I'm here," the Master said.

"I know," the *brujo* answered, gathering his courage to turn and face the dark void that was his Master's face.

The *brujo* looked into emptiness—an infinity of emptiness. He did not dwell on the thought, for he knew such emptiness was his fate once the Master decided he no longer needed him in his physical form.

"The white magic is strong among you humans," the Master said.

"I have felt it," the *brujo* answered. "But we can work the black magic as well."

"There are not enough of you, not enough humans enjoy the taste of hate as you do," the Master answered. "I have had to rely on deluding the selfish and the weak, those who see good in getting what they want and doing it in the name of the Light."

"Can you not do that now?"

"Of course, but that only works in the physical realm," the Master said. "The weak and the foolish have not the skill nor the strength to work magic."

"What would you have me do?"

"Kill," the Master answered. "Kill those who call humanity to the white magic."

"Who and where?"

"I shall guide you," the Master answered, "But there is a problem. There are four of them, and they have taken haven in a sacred place, a place where you cannot walk. It can only be reached by the pure of heart."

"How shall I reach them?"

"I shall send to you the foolish ones, those who serve with all their heart the lies of my lesser servants." The Master laughed. The sound made the Dark One cringe in fear. "They will bring them to you."

Chapter Fourteen

The Search

Agent Walt Chambers sat in the usually innocuous sedan now halted on a mountain road where the sedan failed not only to be innocuous but also to be the least bit mobile. He and Agent Sam Stern were stuck, pure and simple. On the drive from the nearest town, the agents had already expressed regret at their choice of vehicle borrowed from the FBI car pool out of Denver. The state highway had changed to county blacktop to a maintained dirt surface to a narrow road where vehicles going opposite directions had to slow and ease past each other to ensure both vehicles had room to pass. At some points, the trees were so close to the road that there was not room to pass, and one vehicle or the other had to back to the nearest wide spot. All in all, Walt would have preferred the Beltway at five p.m., and that was before the flash rain that turned the dirt road into a surface with a strong resemblance to oatmeal.

It was their fourth day in the New Mexico backwoods. Walt had been fighting inner demons much of the time. The rural areas, the back roads— there were times he felt he was eight-years-old again, back on his grandfather's Alabama farm, sharing space with his younger aunts and uncles in the sharecropper shack that was the family home. His father had left rural

Alabama for Mobile where it was easier to find work, and Walt had taken the migration one step farther when he went to the University of Georgia on a basketball scholarship. ROTC had supplemented the scholarship, and he had somehow drifted into intelligence, more because the Army needed intelligence officers than because of any real interest in the field. Luck of the draw had continued for Walt as his required tour of duty neared an end, and a senior officer told him of the FBI's active recruitment of people of color. A strange combination of determination and inertia had determined the direction of Walt's life. Determination had carried him through his education and out of the poverty that still claimed much of his extended family. Inertia had carried him into a field that he found rewarding but had been no part of any life-dream. That was not totally true.

Respect—he had always dreamed of being treated with respect.

He had watched his grandfather stand, hat-in-hand, while a White man told him he was not welcome in his store. He had watched his father, an accomplished carpenter, obey instructions from a White man half his age whose only qualification was that he was the son of the company's owner.

Wherever he went, Walt was treated with respect. The now useless sedan was a part of that. So were the dark suit and, most importantly, the FBI identification in the leather wallet resting safely in his jacket pocket.

"Looks like we're going to have to push," Sam said from his place in the passenger seat.

They both looked down at their slick-soled leather shoes and well-pressed suits.

"Someone will come along in a minute," Walt

said. "Besides, we won't be able to push this out by hand. We need someone with a four-wheel-drive to pull us through this low-spot."

"Walt, when we get back to Taos tonight, I really think we can justify a SUV rental on the expense report," Sam said.

"I agree," Walt answered. He reached for his briefcase in the backseat. "I guess we could catch up on paperwork while we're waiting."

Sam took off his suit jacket and rolled it into a pillow. "No offense, Walt, but I think I'll catch up on some sleep." Sam reclined the passenger seat and closed his eyes.

Walt smiled at his partner, envying his ability to sleep anywhere. He pulled the file on Kidwell Brown from his briefcase and reread the passages he'd read fifty times over the past week since he had first received the assignment. Everything was there, including her outstanding service record. Her homosexuality was the only potential blot on that record, but fitness reports from commanding officers and interviews with past shipmates made it quite clear that it had not been a major issue for those with whom she served. One poor fitness report in twenty years of service was amazing. Further investigation found that the officer who had given Kidwell the bad fitness report had been asked to resign. Kidwell had reported him for sexual harassment after enlisted women in his command came to her for advice and protection. Apparently, he deemed sexual favors to be a command perk.

Walt and Sam were there for a simple mission— to learn how Kidwell had known about Desert Lightning before it happened. There had been darker hints. Washington was a frenzy of activity, looking for someone to blame for the worst military failure ever experienced by the United States. Kidwell had possibilities as a recipient in the transfer of that blame.

Walt now had a personal problem. He liked Kidwell. More importantly, he respected her. Her service record, the incredible loyalty he had witnessed in the people he had interviewed. The chief from the fire department where she and her partner volunteered had told him, quite frankly, to go to hell if he thought Kidwell and Anna had done anything wrong. Walt knew as well as he knew anything that this woman would not betray her country.

In recent years, especially the past few months, he had begun to wish he could feel as confident about his own superiors. Walt shook his head, pushing back that thought. He could not go there. He loved his job. He loved his country. He preferred that it would stay that simple. If only there were someone he trusted to ask advice…someone in whose wisdom he believed.

"Tough knowing what to do, ain't it, Walty boy?" a voice said behind him.

Walter turned to look into the backseat and stared directly into the eyes of his grandfather.

"Gramps!" Walt called.

Sam sat up and looked into the back seat.

"Hey Walt, who's the old black man?"

"My grandfather," Walt answered.

"How'd he get here?"

Walt willed his open mouth closed and glanced at his partner. "It's stranger than you think, Sam. Gramps died twelve years ago."

Sam turned as white as Walt would have been if the natural melanin in his skin had allowed that to happen.

"You say he's dead?"

"Dead and long buried," Gramps answered for Walt. "Look pretty dang good for the decomposed, don't I?"

"You see him, too?" Walt asked Sam.

"Clear as day."

Tears welled in Walt's eyes. Whatever was happening, he was glad to see his grandfather.

"Gramps, it's good to see you."

"I'm with you often, Walty," the old man said in a gentle voice. "You just don't know it."

Tears spilled onto Walt's checks.

"Why can I see you now?"

"'Cause you wished for me, and 'cause you need to do somethin' important," Gramps answered.

"What?"

"You leave them two girls be," Gramps said. "They got work to do that's bigger than you or the folks what's boss you around."

"Kidwell Brown and Anna Montoya, you mean?" Sam asked.

"None other."

"Are we dreaming?" Sam asked his partner.

Gramps reached forward with the cane that Walt remembered as his constant companion in his later years. He thumped Walt on the right shoulder and then Sam on his left.

"I don't think so," Walt answered.

"You'd better be listening to my friend George here," a new voice said from the back seat.

Sam turned to look directly into the eyes of his grandfather, the one who had died when he was fourteen.

"Grandpa," Sam called.

"Hello, little Sam. You've grown to be a fine, strong fella."

"Grandpa," Sam said again, choking on unexpected tears. He wiped at his eyes with the sleeve of his shirt.

"If you don't listen, we just might have to whip you both," Gramps said, but his voice was different, stronger.

The two agents turned to look at their deceased grandfathers once again. They saw two strapping young men where two old men had sat a moment earlier. They saw their beloved grandfathers as they had been during their prime.

Walt and Sam looked at each other, confirming their shared amazement. When they looked again to the backseat, it was empty of any occupants.

"I…I don't think we should put this in our reports, do you?" Sam said.

"Only if we want an express ticket out of the Bureau."

At that moment, a drab green Forestry Service pickup truck appeared behind them. The driver got out of the truck, and Walt recognized Gene Griego, the director of the local USDA Forestry Division and yet another close friend of Kidwell and Anna. Their interview with Griego had been particularly testy. Gene leaned into Walt's open window.

"Aren't you two through harassing good citizens?" Gene asked.

"You know, Ranger Griego, I think we are done with our job here. Don't you agree, Agent Stern?" Walter said.

"Yes, I do."

Griego looked confused. "What?"

"We have come to the conclusion that Kidwell

Brown and Anna Montoya have been missing for over eight weeks. We presume they died in some unfortunate accident while on a pack trip deep into the National Forest. We believe locating their remains to be the responsibility of the U.S. Forestry Service working with state and local agencies as you deem appropriate."

A broad smile brightened Griego's face. "My office will be happy to conduct any search necessary."

"Then we will leave it in your capable hands. Now, would you mind pulling us out of this mud hole, so we can head back to the regional office in Denver?"

"My pleasure."

Gonzales went one step further. Once he had tugged their mired sedan out of the mud, he followed them all the way back to the nearest highway.

Chapter Fifteen

The Battle

Gunnery Sergeant Tom Smithson felt at home in his Battle Dress Uniform (BDU). The former Marine missed the familiar feel of the heavy cloth. He had thought he would never again go to battle in the forest green BDUs they'd usually worn on base. Every other real battle he had known involved the mottled tan and brown of the desert camouflage. Even more surprising was that he faced real combat on American soil. He felt ecstatic at the opportunity to fight the real enemies of the good old U.S. of A. He had watched the liberals take the name of God out of his kids' school, and he had watched the nation slowly accept the contamination of the sanctity of marriage by allowing queers to join man to man and woman to woman. Smithson had been willing to fight and die for his country. He was willing to fight and die for his God. It had been a relief when Rev. Putnam called him to his office and told him about their secret mission. Sergeant Smithson kept that secret as surely as he did any top-secret battle information. Not even his wife knew the plan. As far as she was concerned, Smithson was elk hunting.

After twelve years in the Marines, Smithson declined to re-up his enlistment after he was saved during a Pentecostal revival at a church near Camp

Lejeune. His kids had gone to the church for Bible School, and his wife had become friends with one of the women there. They had taken the invitation to the revival service as a social invitation. It had been the changing moment in his life.

Smithson ate the preacher's words like a starving man. The passion and fervor of the preacher made his blood quicken, and the man told him all the things he already believed. Smithson was overjoyed as that preacher made it clear that those beliefs were truly the will of God. When the altar call came, Smithson went with the others. He was amazed at his own tears as he prayed with the flock of repentant souls. Rev. Putnam had been at his side that night, and Smithson knew, from that moment on, he would follow the Reverend wherever he wanted him to go.

It had strained his marriage. Jean, his wife and mother of their two children, had not liked Rev. Putnam, and she was uncomfortable with some of the church's teachings, but she went. Smithson made sure of that. After all, it was a woman's place to obey her husband.

Now, as he bound the hands of the rag-head woman they had been sent to kidnap, he was overjoyed to be using his skills in war to serve the true God. Jeffers, another converted Marine serving in his advance party, came through the woods, carrying the still form of the Mexican woman that was among the list they were to bring back to Rev. Putnam. Both captured women were drugged. They had used spring-loaded syringes with a strong but non-lethal sedative. Greg also slept, well-drugged, in the lodge he shared with Aisha. Only the women, Rev. Putnam had instructed, and his orders were to be obeyed.

"You were supposed to wait," Smithson hissed. "We were to take her and the other dyke as they slept."

"I caught her over by the latrine," Jeffers answered. "I couldn't pass up the opportunity."

Smithson nodded. "Good call."

"Tough bitch," Jeffers said. "Didn't go out like a light, and she started to scream."

"I didn't hear her."

"I covered her mouth," Jeffers said, "But there was a price."

Jeffers held up his left hand and showed the Gunnery Sergeant the bloody, half-moon shape of the bite mark.

"Did you hurt her?"

"No more than I had to. Just a few bruises."

"Remember, these women aren't the enemy. They're just misguided souls who listened to the Godless liberals."

"Amen," Jeffers responded.

"Rev. Putnam will set them straight."

"The world will be better off once women learn their place."

"Amen," Smithson answered.

Smithson turned to Witherspoon, the third member of their advance group. He had wondered about Witherspoon, an aging Vietnam vet that Rev. Putnam had rescued from a downhill slide into oblivion. Smithson no longer doubted the man, neither his commitment to the cause nor his ability in combat. He moved through the night like a soundless shadow, and he held his M-16 like it was an extension of his own body.

"You two start back with the rag-head and the Mexican. I'll get the third one," Smithson said.

"Careful. Remember, she's a vet."

Smithson snorted in contempt. "A swabby. She won't be a problem."

Witherspoon's hand covered his upper arm like a vice. "When you underestimate, that's when you die."

Smithson felt a chill go down his spine. "Yeah, I won't forget."

Jeffers and Witherspoon each threw a woman over their shoulders and started back through the woods. It was nearly five miles back to the four-wheelers. It would be tough, humping limp bodies through the woods. There had been two other members of their advance team, mercenaries Putnam had hired from somewhere. The job would have been easier if those two had been there to trade off on the load, but they had simply disappeared when they were a mile from Thunder Lake. Jeffers had been two feet behind one of them, and the man had simply been there one moment and gone the next.

Man, oh man, is he good, Jeffers had thought. He had changed his mind when they arrived at the rendezvous site and the man was not there. *The slacker took his advance money and ran,* Jeffers thought.

Smithson watched his companions for a moment before turning back to the camp. He had his destination in sight—the teepee where Kidwell Brown slept.

※ ※ ※ ※

Kidwell was instantly awake. Peter's voice awoke her.

"You're in danger," the voice said. "Act!"

Kidwell sprang to a crouching position beside their bed. Anna was gone, and Kidwell's heart was in her throat at that realization. She swallowed hard, and let animal instinct return her full attention to the moment. She could not save Anna if she could not save herself. Her rifle and pistol lay just a yard away, but neither was loaded. They had felt safe in the haven and there were too many children among the pilgrims. Instinct told her she did not have time to load a weapon. There was just a moment when she wondered if it was right to fight. She reminded herself that, for whatever reason, the spirits had chosen her, a warrior, for this task. She could only be what she was. Kidwell grabbed her hunting knife from the sheath on her pistol belt and retreated to the far corner of the lodge, taking time to wad the blankets on their bed into something that might be mistaken for a human form in the dark.

She waited, but not for long.

A dark form slowly lifted the flap to the teepee, only as far as he needed to make a quick entrance and then lower the flap behind him. Professional, Kidwell thought as she watched him move. She could see the outline of a man in BDUs, a soft camouflage hat on his head and an M-16 in his hand. He crouched low and made his way silently to the empty bed. The man took a moment to assess the form he thought he saw there and then pulled something from his vest. He laid down the M-16, stabbed toward the bed with one hand, and used the other to cover where he expected a mouth to be.

Kidwell moved quickly. He had not yet had time to realize he had just attacked a phantom when he realized he had a knife at his throat.

"Who are you, and where's Anna?" Kidwell demanded.

The man hesitated only a moment before grabbing

for the knife. If Kidwell had truly intended to cut his throat, he would have died then. Instead, he only received a superficial cut to his throat and a deeper wound to the hand he had used to reach for the knife. Kidwell sprang back, facing her opponent. She then used her most practical weapon.

"Danger!" she yelled at the top of her voice. "Danger in the camp! Help!"

The man dove for the flap of the teepee, Kidwell right behind him. She stabbed for his retreating back, hoping to inflict enough wound to stop him. Her primary desire for all the world was to know where Anna had gone and if she was safe. He was her only tie to that information. She could tell by the feel that her knife had struck a Kevlar flack vest, and the man was out the flap and gone before she could breathe.

She stepped into the night and looked around. He was nowhere to be seen. *Special Forces or Marine,* she thought. *Looks like Admiral O'Hare's warning had been too true. But how did they find the lake,* she wondered.

The quiet camp was no longer quiet. Martin was beside her, rifle in hand. Flashlights flayed through the night from the group of tents where the latest wave of pilgrims slept.

"What happened?" Martin asked.

"Peter woke me to tell me I was in danger. Some guy came into our teepee. I think he tried to kill me."

"Where is he?"

"He got away, but I drew blood. That should help us track him." Kidwell swallowed hard. "Martin, Anna's gone."

Martin looked around. "Where's Greg and Aisha?"

Three pilgrims and their Taos guide now stood

beside them. They were all demanding to know what was happening. Kidwell explained as briefly as she could while they followed her and Martin to Aisha and Greg's lodge. They found Greg unconscious in their bed, the spring-loaded syringe still stuck in his thigh. A second syringe lay beside the bed. Martin pulled the needle from Greg's leg while Kidwell checked his pulse and respiration.

"He's alive," Kidwell said, obvious relief in her voice. She looked at the syringe. "I remember this from Radiological, Biological, and Chemical warfare training, but I don't remember the specifics." She read the contents. "I think it's just a strong sedative. Special Ops guys use these sometimes."

"So you think the Army's after us?" Martin asked.

"I don't know." Kidwell paused for thought. "I think if this had been a sanctioned operation, the military would have sent in overwhelming forces rather than just one guy or maybe a handful of spooks."

"They should not have been here," the Taos guide said. Besides Kidwell and Martin, he and one woman had been the only ones of the visitors to enter the teepee.

Martin nodded agreement. "Why did the spirit protectors let them in?"

"Perhaps they came because they truly believed in what they were doing," Kidwell said.

The pilgrim woman took the syringe from Kidwell and then read the label. "I'm a nurse," the woman said. "You're right, it's a sedative. He should wake up in a couple of hours with a bad case of cotton-mouth."

"Can you take care of Greg?" Kidwell asked the woman.

     Kayt C. Peck

"Of course."

Kidwell stood and moved with purpose out of Aisha and Greg's lodge and toward her own.

"What are you doing?" Martin asked, following close behind her.

"Getting my weapons. I'm going after them."

Martin put his hand on her shoulder, halting her progress. Kidwell turned to look at him. "It will be daylight in an hour," Martin said. "We can track them then. If we head out now, we may cover up the very tracks we need to find them."

Kidwell chewed at her lip, knowing he was right. "Martin." Her voice cracked. "They have Anna."

Martin pulled her to him and hugged her until her ribs ached. "We'll get her back," he promised.

Kidwell choked back tears and pushed herself away. "We have two horses in the pens. The others should come if we shake the feed bucket." She turned to the pilgrims. "Do any of you know how to ride and shoot?"

❧❦❧❦

Gunnery Sergeant Smithson ran low and quiet, using cover wherever he could find it. His hand and throat ached and bled, but he ignored the pain. In a moment's pause, he wrapped a triangular field bandage around his hand, as much to stop the blood trail he was leaving as to treat the injured hand. The dyke had cut him badly. When he glanced at the hand, he could see exposed bone and tendon. For a second, he felt battlefield hate, followed immediately by the physical sickness that had always been his reaction to that hate. He had never told anyone of that reaction, secretly wondering if he had what it took to be a good Marine.

After that brief pause, Smithson ran without pause toward the rendezvous point where the four-wheelers waited. His buddies had a head start, but they were slowed with the burden of carrying two women. He hoped to catch them before they headed back to the camp where Rev. Putnam waited with that other man, the silent, dark man whom the Reverend had simply introduced as a servant of the Lord. Meeting that man had been the only time Smithson had doubted the purpose of their mission, but Rev. Putnam had been certain, with the scripture needed to strengthen Smithson's resolve.

Jeffers and Witherspoon were waiting for him when he arrived at the rendezvous. From their shortness of breath, Smithson guessed they hadn't been there for long. The two women were already loaded onto the cargo racks of two of the ATVs. Smithson stifled a shudder as he realized just how much they reminded him of carrying freshly killed deer. One woman, the Mexican, moaned quietly. The drug was beginning to wear off. The three men shared water from one canteen.

"Where's the other woman?" Jeffers asked.

Smithson looked directly at Witherspoon and raised his hand for his companions to see the blood and the bandage. "The swabby was tougher than I expected, and she was ready for me. God knows what warned her."

"We can't go back without her. Remember, she was the one the Reverend wanted the most," Jeffers said.

Witherspoon smiled coldly and looked at Anna, where she was tied to the vehicle like a slab of meet. "Don't worry, she'll come."

"Yes, she will," Smithson said. "We need to get these two to the Reverend and set up an ambush for the other woman."

"She won't be alone. That Indian kid and some of the folks camped with them will probably help," Witherspoon said.

"We have some time. They won't be able to track us 'til daylight and they can't move very fast on foot," Smithson responded.

Smithson thought like a modern fighting man. He forgot about the horses. The oversight could well change the future for all humanity.

❧❧❧❧

The trail was surprisingly easy to follow. Great drops of blood took them to where the intruder had paused in the brush. The amount of blood slowed after that, making Martin and Kidwell suspect that the man had bound his wound, but he made no effort to hide his tracks as he ran through the woods.

"He may have been a professional," Kidwell said, "But he's used to Special Ops strategy. He's been trained to do the job, haul buns out of there, and wait for extraction."

Martin dismounted to look at yet another clear print of a deeply treaded combat boot. "He ain't no Indian. That's for sure."

In less than half a mile, the sole traveler's trail joined the prints of two other sets of combat boots, deeply embedded in the duff and the mud.

"They must be carrying Anna and Aisha," Martin said.

Kidwell scrutinized the trail desperately, her mind

only slightly eased by the lack of blood. She prayed for Anna's safety. For now, it was the best she could do.

Every horse available was mounted. Kidwell rode her appaloosa and Martin rode his paint. The Taos guide had Anna's mare and two of the pilgrims, one man and one woman, rode Greg and Aisha's horses. So far, no one had slowed the group. The pilgrims had included a couple from Minneapolis who had shared the same dream on the same night when their teenage son, killed two years ago in an auto accident, had told them they were needed at the Taos reservation in New Mexico. Another group was a mix of ranchers and shopkeepers from Conchas, New Mexico. They were friends of the cowboy who had shown up confused and a tad frightened – riding an oversized ATV – the day after Peter had left the urn.

The cowboy had been checking cattle near his home when he paused for a noontime nap. He awoke 150 miles north of where he had gone to sleep, within sight of the Thunder Lake campsite. They fed him lunch and told their story. In the afternoon, they carefully loaded the urn on the cowboy's ATV, padding it meticulously with pine boughs, and sent him on his way. Kidwell sent the urn to a friend, an ex-priest whom she still knew to be a holy man. He would know what to do with the precious documents.

Kidwell had been glad of the gift of the cowboy when he had arrived that day. She was even more thankful for the gift of the pilgrims he had sent to them.

"If they stay a walking, it won't take us long to catch up to them," said the pilgrim Sara McQuirter. She was within spitting distance of sixty, but she sat on her horse as if she was born to it, and she held Kidwell's rifle as if she meant business. Kidwell carried the M-16 that the intruder had abandoned in her teepee. The pistol and knife strapped at her side made her by far the best armed of the group.

"Not all of this country is like the Thunder Lake area," said McQuirter's young hired hand. "There will be logging roads and jeep trails. There's no guarantee they walked in all the way."

Kidwell's heart sank and Martin glared at the cowhand. "We'll catch them," Martin said. "We're supposed to."

They kept the horses at a walk until they came to the four-wheeler trail where two machines had been abandoned. Kidwell contemplated commandeering the machines, but decided that they could move nearly as fast on the horses and, hopefully, maintain the element of surprise.

Martin studied the tracks around the site. "Looks like five walked in and only three walked out," Martin said. Kidwell felt vindicated at her instructions for those remaining behind to carry Greg to a cave near Thunder Lake and take shelter there. They had left the shotgun and one rifle with the group as well.

"The other two. The guardians stopped them," the Taos guide said.

Kidwell looked at the man. There was a ring of truth to his words. Her heart felt a hint of relief amid the firestorm of anxiety.

Once on the trail, Martin took point, riding ahead of the group and acting as a scout. Kidwell rode about fifty yards behind him with the other three twenty yards behind her. If there was trouble, Martin would see it first. Even if Kidwell did not have time to react, the rest of the party should have hope of escape or effective confrontation. They picked up their pace considerably. The trail of the ATVs could be easily followed at a fast trot or even a lope.

They had gone several miles when Martin halted, signaling for silence as the others approached. He led the group off the trail and into the woods. Once they reached a low point not visible from the trail, he dismounted and tied his horse to a tree limb. The others followed suit. They gathered in a group to listen to Martin's whispered report.

"We're close. There's still water seeping into a track at that last water crossing, and I saw a small column of wood smoke over the next ridge. I think we're near a campsite."

"This is the plan," Kidwell instructed. "Martin and I are going to take point. I want the rest of you to form a line about ten yards to our rear with ten to fifteen feet between each person. We'll recon what we can see over that ridge and then re-group for a battle plan if it truly is the campsite."

Kidwell taught the group a series of simple hand signals—move forward, halt, fall back and re-group, stand fast. No one questioned her command. They simply did as instructed.

❧❧❧❧

Smithson understood neither Spanish nor Arabic, but he was absolutely certain that the two women tied to the ATVs were not calling him names that he would want repeated to his children. He was amazed that neither woman begged for mercy. The trip alone had to be miserable. They were tied to bare metal, and the trail was rough and unforgiving. He knew there would be bruises to show for the journey. In truth, he wished he had time to stop and make them more comfortable, but that would not have been a wise combat decision. He led the party directly to Rev. Putnam's camp. When they stopped the ATVs, Putnam rushed from his tent, a tent that contained everything from an air mattress to a porta-potty to make the trip bearable for the Reverend. He was not accustomed to outdoor living.

"There are only two," the Reverend said.

"The other one raised the camp before we had a chance to nab her," Smithson responded.

The Dark One strode from where he had been resting in the dark of the woods. He gruffly grasped the hair of Aisha and then Anna, looking into each of their faces.

"Where's the warrior?" he demanded.

"Don't worry. She'll follow. The dyke won't let us take her partner without a fight. We need to make a plan," Jeffers said.

The Dark One turned his attention back to the women still tied to the ATVs. "Waiting can be pleasant," he said.

Smithson's blood beat coldly through his veins. "What do you mean?"

The Dark One turned blue eyes as cold as emptiness toward Smithson. "Can't you guess?"

The Dark One pulled a Bowie knife, old and well sharpened, from the sheath on his belt. He sliced the rope that tied Aisha to the ATV, lifted her with one hand, and then dumped her unceremoniously on the ground. When he did the same to Anna, the Latina managed to land one strong bite on his forearm. He responded with a blow to her face that nearly knocked her unconscious.

"Hey! There's no call for that," Smithson said. He

turned to Rev. Putnam. "Reverend. Who is this man?"

A wild look filled Putnam's eyes. "The voice of God said to trust him." The soft and spoiled preacher looked at the women with a hunger, a fire. "The voice of God says these women deserve what they get for daring to blaspheme the Holy Scriptures."

Smithson felt a fear unlike anything he had ever known before. "The voice of God?"

The preacher looked at his follower. "I finally heard it. All my life I've prayed for it. The voice sent me here and bid me do his will."

Smithson looked at the Dark One as he towered over the women. "Reverend, are you sure that voice was from God?"

Although they were no longer bound to the ATVs, both Anna and Aisha still had their hands tied. The Dark One grabbed Aisha by the rope around her wrists and lifted her to a sitting position. He grabbed at her blouse and ripped it away in a single motion, exposing her breasts.

"Stop!" Smithson yelled. Jeffers and Witherspoon added their cries to his.

"This isn't right," Jeffers demanded.

The Rev. Putnam laughed a laugh that made Smithson feel sick to his stomach. The preacher stared wide-eyed at Aisha's exposed breasts. "Deserve what they get…voice of God," the preacher mumbled.

Jeffers stepped forward and grabbed the Dark One by the shoulder. "Leave these women alone," he demanded.

In one fluid motion, the Dark One plunged the Bowie knife deep into Jeffers' stomach, thrusting upward, toward the heart. Jeffers' face expressed the mother of all surprise.

"No!" Smithson and Witherspoon called in unison. Smithson drew his 9mm from the holster on his belt, and Witherspoon ran for the M-16 in the scabbard on his ATV. Smithson fired three rounds into the Dark One, watching the man jerk as each bullet hit.

There was a moment's pause. The Dark One didn't fall. Instead, he turned to face Smithson. As Smithson watched, the three bloody holes in the man's shirt simply disappeared, like the invisible ink Smithson had used as a kid.

"Jesus help us," Witherspoon cried. He dropped the M-16 back in its scabbard, and added to the pandemonium by firing up his ATV. He rode like he knew his life depended on it.

Rev. Putnam dropped to the ground, curled in a fetal position. A puddle appeared below him, followed by the smell of urine.

The Dark One pulled the knife from Jeffers' already dead body, and turned toward Smithson. Smithson emptied the pistol into his attacker, but each bullet only deepened the man's hateful excuse for a smile.

"Dear God, what have I done?" Smithson said. He thought about running, but felt it would be fruitless. He would rather die facing his enemy.

The Dark One raised the knife, and Smithson spit in his face. The smile turned to a sneer. Just before the blade came down, surely with enough strength to sever Smithson head, he heard the familiar pop of an M-16, and a small, round hole appeared in the Dark One's forehead. It disappeared just as the others had done, but the Dark One looked beyond Smithson to the hill behind him.

"He's not who you came for, is he?" a voice

shouted. "If you want me, you'll have to come and get me."

Smithson turned and looked up the hill. Kidwell Brown stood there, an M-16 in her hands. The Dark One pushed Smithson aside and started up the hill. Kidwell ran as if the devil himself was after her. Perhaps he was.

A decoy, Smithson thought. She's using herself as a decoy.

※ ※ ※ ※

Kidwell had expected time to create a plan, mount a coordinated rescue effort. Such was not the case. She and Martin peeked over the edge of the ridge just as the huge, dark-haired man dumped Anna onto the ground. Never in her life had Kidwell exerted as much self-control as when he backhanded her lover for the bite she inflicted. Martin held her arm so tightly he left bruises, but there had been no need. Kidwell sat silent and still, drawing her own blood as she bit her lip. Kidwell had motioned for the others to move up and then motioned for them to stand fast once they reached positions at the top of the ridge. She watched in amazement at what unfolded below, as the soldiers who kidnapped Anna and Aisha now stood in their defense. She watched as one man died and the Dark One took bullets as if they were stones from a slingshot.

As the Dark One prepared to kill the second man, Kidwell acted as much from instinct as from planning.

"I'll provide a diversion," she hissed at Martin. "Stay low until I draw him away."

Kidwell popped over the ridge and fired a perfect shot into the Dark One's head. Whatever hope she had that a head wound might finish him disappeared as she watched the wound evaporate.

"He's not the one you came for, is he?" she yelled. "If you want me, you'll have to come and get me."

Kidwell ran as she had never run in her life. She had at least a twenty-yard head start on the big demon of a man, but she knew it was not enough.

"Spirit, help me," she prayed silently, saving her breath for the run.

Kidwell dropped the rifle, knowing it was useless against the man behind her and would slow her run. If he killed her, she hoped it would satisfy his blood lust. She hoped he would leave, leave Anna and the others alive.

They ran into the woods. Based on the super human traits she had already witnessed, Kidwell suspected it wouldn't take him long to catch her. As she ran, she studied the land around her, choosing her ground for a fight. She jumped to a boulder with a relatively flat top, pulled her pistol, and turned to face him. He stopped and laughed at her effort at defense.

"My Master sent me to kill you," he said.

"And mine sent me to live as best I could."

He laughed again. "I wish I had time to make you suffer." He brandished the Bowie knife. "But I'd better get this job finished."

Kidwell emptied her .357 into his hulking form, with the same effect as all the other shots. He jumped to the boulder and slashed with the knife, Kidwell jumped back, but the knife left a slash across her shoulder and chest. It burned even more than a cut should. She shifted the revolver to her left hand, using it to block another thrust of the Bowie knife, all while she reached for the knife on her belt with her right. To her surprise, what she grasped was not the knife, but the hilt of a Celtic sword, one that felt like an old friend to her hand. Kidwell pulled the sword and the Dark One backed away, nearly falling from the boulder, shading his eyes from the light emanating from the blade.

"Nasty bitch," the Dark One screamed. "How dare you?" In two hundred years, it was the first time a human had matched his dark magic with white. He was uncertain.

Kidwell saw the opportunity. She kept her high ground and slashed at the man below her. As blade met blade, Kidwell saw that his knife had transformed as well. He now held a long sword, exceeding her own in length by at least three inches. His sword was a dark metal that absorbed light in counter-balance to her blade's radiation of light. The sound when the two blades met exceeded the clank of metal one would expect from a normal sword fight. There was an echo, a ring that the soul as well as the ears could hear. With a couple of parries, Kidwell realized that she had the advantage. Not only did she have the high ground, but she realized that her memories of time as a Celtic warrior gave her superior abilities over the inexperienced swordsman fighting from below her. She saw fear in his eyes and suspected that was the first real fear the Dark One had known for a very, very long time. Her only disadvantage was the cut to her shoulder and chest. It was not deep, but she felt darkness in it, draining her of strength and determination. She must act fast before it worsened.

She attacked with three blows in rapid succession, nearly knocking the man to his knees. The Dark One retreated, going beyond her reach from her high ground on the boulder. He stood with sword raised, wide-eyed and confused. Kidwell debated whether to give up her high ground advantage and waited briefly, hoping he would step in to attack again. That's when she was hit from behind.

It was horrifying, the physical contact with the unseen assailant. It was as if she had touched evil itself. In truth, she had. The blow didn't knock her down, but it did force her to jump, unbalanced from her high ground advantage. She glanced at the new assailant and saw a flying shadow with no specific features, the outlined darkness of what she knew to be a demon. The Dark One grasped the opportunity and slashed at Kidwell. She lifted her blade and deflected the blow, raising her left hand holding the pistol as some small protection against the flying demon. To her surprise, the pistol was gone. In its place was a round shield. When the demon attacked again, the shield easily deflected the negative energy. Both the demon and the Dark One backed away, assessing these unexpected changes. In that instant, Kidwell glanced at her shield, surprised to see not the traditional cross she expected but the Tree of Life, the symbol of the Goddess. She felt White Buffalo Calf Woman's hand in this new tool.

Kidwell jumped back to her boulder, feeling that as long as her strength held, there was hope. That hope did not last long. As she watched, a black vortex formed and ten more featureless demons flew into the clearing. At that point, Kidwell ceased her silent prayer to win the battle. Instead, she prayed for the salvation of her very soul in the face of such evil.

The demons and the Dark One attacked as one. Using shield and sword, Kidwell moved in a whirlwind, hearing the screams as her blade connected with the demons. She had no hope that they could be killed, but she saw two dissipate in a noxious smoke as her blade severed head from body. It took all she had to fend off that first assault from so many. The next would be her last. She knew that.

Suddenly Martin was there, between Kidwell and the Dark One. She had no clue how he had come to be there, and she looked with hope at the weapon he carried. Martin brandished a smoldering bundle of sacred sage. The Dark One's confidence evaporated. The other demons hovered at a safe distance. Kidwell turned, standing back-to-back with Martin. Then the others were there; Anna was at her side, holding her own smoldering sage, with the rancher Sara McQuirter defending Kidwell's left, sage held high before her. The Dark One wanted Kidwell, but Martin moved too quickly, staying between Kidwell and the leader of the devilish squad.

"Stupid Indian," the Dark One said as he thrust toward Martin with the sword. Amazingly, the sage burned a large bite from the lethal blade. As Martin occupied the Dark One, the others managed to keep the demons at a distance.

The Dark One feinted with the sword, and Martin moved with the sage. This time the sage touched flesh on the Dark One's arm, causing him to scream in pain. With his other hand, the Dark One used his fist to hit Martin full in the face. The young Apache collapsed in a heap. Kidwell stood, waiting for the Dark One's next attack. He looked at the sword in her hand and laughed that dark laugh that was really beginning to annoy Kidwell.

"Haven't you learned by now? No human can kill me!"

The Dark One lunged, and Kidwell deflected his

sword with her own. She jabbed the edge of her shield into his face, and he screamed in pain at the touch of the sacred shield. Kidwell plunged her blade deep into the Dark One's chest.

"Somehow, I think you're wrong," Kidwell said, her face just inches from the Dark One's cold blue eyes.

The plain steel of the blade disappeared in her hand and the sword became the blade of light it had been when held in the angel's hand. A transformation took place in the Dark One's face as he stood dying. The cold blue of his eyes took on warmth. The shock turned to pain.

"My name…my name was Nathan," the Dark One said.

He looked directly at Kidwell. "I see you, Nathan," she said, feeling a certainty that the devil was gone and the man had returned.

Nathan's eyes lost focus, and he looked into nowhere. "Oh, my God, what have I done?"

❧❧❧❧

When the human who had once been immortal collapsed, Kidwell pushed herself away. The sword of light disappeared, turning back into her knife, and the shield again became her pistol. The body lying at her feet transformed, progressing through two hundred years of decomposition in two hundred seconds. The body lay on the rocky ground, a mound of dust in a human shape.

All of the members of her rescue party, along with Aisha and the former Marine, Smithson, now stood around Kidwell, brandishing their sage. The Taos guide held a small hand drum, and he began to play. As he did, the demons flew in a frenzy of pain. The vortex opened again, and they rushed within, escaping to their darkness until the opening closed with a resounding snap. It was over, at least for now.

Kidwell fell to her knees. The wound on her shoulder and chest already stank of rot.

"A wound from a devil blade," Kidwell said to herself.

Martin struggled to his feet, shaking his head. He looked at the pile of dust that had been the Dark One.

"It's over," he said, relief in his voice.

Kidwell looked up at him, beads of sweat on her forehead. "Yes, it's over."

Martin looked at Kidwell and dropped to one knee. "How bad is it?"

"I think…I think it was no ordinary blade." She dropped to her knees. "I'm so cold," she said softly.

"Kidwell!" Anna screamed. She knelt beside her lover.

"He got me, honey," Kidwell said.

Anna took Kidwell in her arms, and Kidwell gratefully leaned against her. The pain had begun to lessen. Kidwell suspected that was not a good sign.

"Stand aside, Anna," Aisha said.

Everyone looked to Aisha, who now held an embroidered bag.

"What's that?" Martin asked.

"A gift from the Prophet's wife," Aisha answered.

Kidwell could no longer hold herself up, even on her knees. Anna helped ease her to a position lying on her side. Aisha dipped deep within the salve and spread the healing mixture on Kidwell's wound. The foul smell disappeared within moments, and Kidwell felt life returning to her body. Anna held her close, and they both cried with relief.

"Do you think that stuff might work on my friend? Do you think…do you think it might bring him back?" Smithson asked.

Aisha looked up at the former Marine.

"I'm really sorry we kidnapped you," Smithson said. "We thought we were doing God's will. The Reverend said…"

Aisha turned her attention to the deep purple bruise on Anna's face. She placed her finger in the salve and traced it along Anna's face. The swelling lessened, and the purple disappeared.

"It might work," Aisha said. She stood and looked Smithson in the face. "And I believe in forgiveness."

Chapter Sixteen

The World

Senator Laura Fletcher looked at the items on her desk like a detective studying clues. Two spiral-bound books, a letter, and a piece of pending health-care legislation lay in a neat semicircle. Florescent Post-It notes marked sections in each book and the letter was worn from where it had been read and reread.

The books were not professionally printed nor bound. Each cover held a simple title and nothing else. One was entitled *The Book of Kidwell* and the other was *The Book of Aisha*. She had read about the books in waves of emails from the New Age set included in her constituency. The Senator had paid little heed, assuming they were another crackpot trend. Then she met Jeffers.

Jeffers had been a part of her campaign team during the last election, and he was invited to one of her regular receptions arranged by her campaign professionals whenever she returned to her district. The man had changed. She remembered him vaguely as part of the Putnam group. Senator Fletcher had never liked Rev. Putnam, but he had an uncanny ability to bring in the conservative vote, so she had attempted to keep relations cordial. She felt little grief when she lost Putnam's support after she abstained from voting on legislation about partial-birth abortion. In general, she agreed with the conservative stand on abortion, but she had heard convincing testimony from physicians about the rare and real medical need for partial-birth abortion.

Opponents of the practice made it sound as though it were a method of birth control. It was not. Case examples included rare instances when mothers carried partially formed fetuses full term if medical intervention did not terminate the pregnancy. This could be extremely hazardous to the mother. She remembered one particularly moving testimony from a mother who carried a fetus that never developed a brain. The family was poor and had not sought medical care from a public clinic until well into the pregnancy. Once she learned that the fetus within her was not fully a baby, the woman was forced to carry the fetus another four weeks before medical professionals were able to jump through all the legal hoops necessary for her to receive a late term abortion. Besides the physical risk (it was hard to predict when the fetus would become dead tissue), it was mental and emotional agony. The woman and her husband spent four weeks mourning the death of a child that she still carried within her. Laura was a hardened legislator, having spent eight years as a state congresswoman before seeking national office, but she still lay awake at night, wrestling with her opposition to abortion and her memory of the weeping face of that still mourning mother. She had abstained. It was the best answer she could find.

The rabid letters she had received from Putnam and others of his ilk had not only lost her many conservative votes but also expressed damnation for her eternal soul. On a personal level, Laura felt relief to finally be rid of the need to appease such adamant radicals. On a professional level, she feared for her political life.

Because of his association with Putnam, Jeffers had triggered real fear for the Senator when she saw the man standing in line at the reception for her political supporters. She looked anxiously at the books he carried and secretly wondered how easy it would be to disguise a bomb as a book. The Senator swallowed her fear and greeted the young man with a large smile and a warm handshake.

"Jeffers, isn't it?" the Senator said. "So, how's your Rev. Putnam?"

Jeffers blushed deeply. "Not well," he answered. "He's currently at the state mental hospital; otherwise he'd be in jail. Over twenty young women and girls have stepped forward to testify that he sexually abused them over the past fifteen years."

The Senator could not fully contain a smug smile. *I always knew the man was a creep*, she thought.

"I'm very sorry to hear that," she said.

"Senator, I'm extremely embarrassed by my affiliation with Putnam."

"He must be a great embarrassment to all his followers."

Jeffers laughed and shook his head. "You'd be amazed at how many people still support him and refuse to believe the truth."

The Senator had been around a long time. "I've seen that happen before."

Those waiting in line behind Jeffers were beginning to glare, and a man not far behind him cleared his throat loudly. Jeffers glanced at the man and spoke rapidly.

"Senator, I would very much appreciate a few minutes of your time. I have some information that I think could be important for you."

Laura looked into the man's eyes, weighing his motivation and purpose.

"All right," she said, hesitantly. "There's a room here we can use for a few minutes. Wait around until I'm finished with the reception line."

"Thank you, Senator."

Jeffers moved forward, making space for the Senator to shake the next hand. On the surface, the Senator gave each person her full attention, but she was constantly aware of Jeffers, books still under his arm and a cup of punch in his other hand. At one point, she paused to motion for her chief of security. She whispered a question to him about the books Jeffers held.

"Just some crazy New Age stuff," the man whispered back. "We've been watching him, but I don't think he's a risk."

"I'm meeting with him after I greet the last person in line. I don't want you in the room with us, but stay close," she instructed.

"Yes, ma'am."

The Senator's heart raced as she led Jeffers to a small meeting room near the reception hall. She glanced down the hall, assuring herself that security personnel were close by, before she closed the door.

Jeffers' story amazed her. He wasted no time getting to the point. Initially, she had found it simply entertaining, and she had willingly taken the books from him, deciding to read bits and pieces out of sheer curiosity. A year earlier, she would have dismissed him immediately as a nut case, but no one in Washington was as certain of anything since Desert Lightning. He must have seen the skepticism in her face because he asked if he could show her his scars.

The Senator laughed, embarrassed, but too curious to say no. Jeffers removed his jacket and opened his shirt. A sharp intake of breath was the Senator's only response. There should have been no scars to show. The man had been eviscerated.

"You should be dead," she said.

"I was."

The Senator dropped into a nearby chair. "What do you mean?"

"I was raised from the dead, Senator, by the hand of the very woman I'd kidnapped and turned over to Putnam."

"I want to hear this story."

Jeffers reached over and tapped the cover of the books the Senator now held. "It's all in there," Jeffers said.

The Senator raised the books and really looked at them for the first time.

"This should be some interesting reading," she said.

"Senator, there's some very interesting living that went into those books."

The Senator surprised herself as she told Jeffers to give her secretary his contact information. She had a feeling they might be talking again.

On the flight home, the Senator had opened *The Book of Kidwell,* looking forward to something amusing as a break from the reams of testimony and legislation that was her usual reading material. Before she had finished the introduction, she was hooked. Kidwell Brown used the first five pages to list her every flaw and every failing.

"I'm nothing special," Kidwell wrote. "I'm just a human being who asked for guidance and listened when it was given to me. As you read these pages, don't make it about me. Make it about you. You can ask for your own guidance. Just don't forget to listen."

The next day, the Senator put in a work order for a nameplate to go on her desk. "Don't forget to listen," was all it said. The print shop had since told her secretary that they had received at least a dozen orders duplicating that desk-plate. Without knowing the real purpose or origin, senators and their staff throughout the building were picking up the saying. The Senator was glad. In some small way, maybe it would make a difference. When asked about its origin, the Senator had not had the courage to tell anyone that it came from *The Book of Kidwell*. The Senator loved the way Kidwell mixed personal commentary with the telling of what she had seen and experienced in this dimension and in others.

Picking up that same book, the Senator turned to a passage she had tagged with a Post-It and marked in ink. She read it again.

We're still at a loss as to what to do with the pilgrims who find their way to our hideaway. They are supposed to be here or the guardians would not allow them to find the place, but I am frightened when they look to me with worship in their eyes. I'm a stumbling bum just trying to find my own way.

My friend and ally, Aisha, gave me the answer. The revelation came not from a session with her spirit guides. It came from her years as an art teacher. She deals well with the pilgrims. They ask her for answers, and, instead, she asks questions, guiding their minds, hearts, and souls to find their own solutions.

Watching her helped me find an answer of my own. Spiritual growth isn't a science. It's an art. An art teacher could tell a student to draw a line this way, give formulas to mix colors and provide paint-by-number pictures to reproduce exactly, but the end product would be something less than art, and the student would have learned nothing but to regurgitate what the teacher gave them.

The soul is one amazing canvas, and no one can paint the art truly waiting there but the person entrusted with that canvas.

Those willing to give answers and striving to stifle questions that take people outside the box of their answers have corrupted our world. They want them to believe. Is there any great, any truly massive evil committed in the history of humanity that did not have its origins in self-serving individuals who disguised their own wishes as the voice of God? What's more, the lies they create outlive the people who create them. This can only happen when enough people hand over the canvas of their soul to the hands of painters who disguise the true nature of what it is they wish to create.

Aisha and I are working together and separately to pass on something that's been given to us. As you read these pages, never forget that it is simply a description of my journey, not a roadmap for your own.

It is a step of faith, giving up the need to know what is right for anyone but yourself. The mosaic of humanity is complex. I believe (it may or may not be true for you) that when I find myself in opposition to another, we may both be right. Even if I must oppose them, I cannot judge them. Their canvas is their own to paint, not mine.

The Senator glanced at *The Book of Aisha*. She found the passages almost as beautiful as the color templates of the author's art mixed in the pages, but it did not speak to her as strongly as *The Book of Kidwell*. Perhaps it was because the Senator came from a Christian background, as did Kidwell. Although she could not understand them, the Senator rejoiced at the passages in Arabic mixed with the pages in English. It gave her hope. Perhaps Aisha's message would touch more of the world.

Next was the letter from a constituent. She received hundreds, but this one had caught her by the throat and held her. Her staff had laid the letter on her desk along with a dozen others because it dealt with health-care, one of the crucial subjects currently under debate.

The letter was simple, written in the broad hand of a woman unaccustomed to the use of the written word with English obviously her second language. She was the widow of a migrant farm worker, a man who had made his living, raised their children, and lived his life harvesting onions and potatoes. He had died of pneumonia. Death came in the bedroom of a humble migrant shack. No hospital would take him. They had not lived in the county long enough to qualify for indigent care. At the emergency room a week before, the doctors had decided her husband could make the trip back to their permanent residence for care. The woman did not have the courage to tell them that they had no way of making that journey. Their eldest son had hitchhiked five hundred miles to be by her side. He was at the hospital, fighting to have his father admitted while the man simply slipped away, nestled in the arms of his wife.

Tears welled in the eyes of the hardened legislator. She felt powerless at the turn of events in the current health-care debate. Champions for various lobbying groups – primarily pharmaceutical companies and health services – dominated the discussion. AARP was making some good points for elder care, but no one was being paid to speak for the indigent. No lobbyist had a high paying expense account to use on their behalf. No group had the funds for the huge campaign donations so necessary for re-election. The Senator knew that she played the game, just as they all did. It had become a necessary evil, but the process sickened her, made it impossible to commit herself fully to serving the people as she had dreamed when she was a young idealist.

The Senator leaned back in her chair and closed her eyes.

"What can I do?" she said, to no one in particular.

"I had a dream," a voice said from across her desk.

The Senator opened her eyes and looked directly at Martin Luther King, Jr. He sat in the chair across from her.

She fought to breathe. "Dr. King!"

"I did not live to see my dream come to life, but I had a dream, and I shared that dream."

"What are you saying?"

"Woman, name me your dream," Dr. King said.

The Senator thought. "I dream that we can create legislation that means no one must die because they can't afford healthcare."

Dr. King laughed. His eyes softened as he looked at her.

"That's not a dream. That's a goal. Name me

your dream."

The Senator closed her eyes, looking deep within her heart, searching for the dream. Tears streamed down her cheeks, pain and joy mixing as she dug within the storage chest of her heart and dusted off old thoughts and hopes.

"I dream…I dream of a time when the decisions of the nation will be made of the people, for the people, and by the people."

King smiled. "That, my friend, is a dream." He leaned forward and tapped the pending legislation on her desk. "Start here, but keep your focus on the dream."

The civil rights legend stood, turned, and walked with purpose toward the closed door, where he simply disappeared. The Senator looked first at the desk-plate: "Don't forget to listen." She looked then at the legislation before her. No lobbyist had approached her to speak for the indigent.

She would anyway. Re-election be damned. She would do her job.

Chapter Seventeen

Home

It had taken over two weeks to find their haven at Thunder Lake when the companions first became refugees. It took fewer than six days to make their way home again. True, knowing their end destination from the very beginning shortened the journey, but that was not the primary reason for the shortened journey. Even the animals were eager to be on their way. The first night, they had planned on making camp early so they did not push the animals too hard on the first day. After finding a site, they started to dismount, but all the animals danced and snorted. As she went to lift the pannier from his back, Sam the mule launched an energetic kick in Kidwell's general direction that could have been lethal if he had seriously tried to connect. Kidwell launched a kick of her own into the mule's side (having learned early that Sam needed a stern hand, or boot as the case may be) and then turned to her companions, who were also having difficulty with their animals.

"Hold on, folks. If our mounts still feel this good, I say we do a few more miles," Kidwell said.

No one argued. They all wanted to go home.

Home…home is where the heart is, they (whoever that may be) say. Their mountain cabin had been home for Anna and Kidwell for several years. Oddly enough, the little mountain area where the two women lived had nudged its way into filling the home slot in the hearts of Aisha and Greg as well. Even Martin, who had never laid eyes on the place, felt a great excitement as they rode toward "home."

During the winter months, Anna made the arduous journey three times from Thunder Lake down to the Taos Pueblo. She rode on the back of a snowmobile with one of their Native American hosts. The two-day journey in the cold was undertaken for a single purpose. Anna had to make her regular phone call to her "uncle," Admiral John O'Hare.

The first winter call had been like her summer conversations, pleasant exchanges about health and weather and subtle messages that things were about the same. The second effort had been frightening. No answer, despite the fact she had called nearly every hour on the hour all evening and then the next morning until the time she had to climb on the snowmobile and make the arduous journey back to camp. Neither Admiral O'Hare nor Master Chief Franconi had answered her calls. Kidwell, who had traveled with Anna on that excursion, had been even more anxious than her mate. During the weeks that followed, they asked their Taos hosts to bring copies of the *Washington Post* whenever possible, and Kidwell had studied each section carefully, looking for any clue of purges within the ranks of the Pentagon's senior officers. Instead, quite the opposite, the news seemed generally positive. It was a mystery.

The third trip down the mountain had been different. The spring thaw had already begun, and Anna and Martin had made the trip on horseback, leaving Kidwell and Aisha to their meditations and Greg to watch the camp. When Anna called the Admiral, all she got was the answering machine, but it was the sweetest message she had ever heard.

"Leave your name and number after the beep. If this is my niece, Anna, go home. It's time," the machine said.

Neither Anna nor Martin had slept well that night, each anxious to get back to Thunder Lake and share the news with their companions. The group responded just as they had expected. It had taken only two days for them to prepare the haven for their departure. What food and wood they had not used, except for what was needed for the journey home, they had carefully stored, leaving it for the Taos and other Pueblos who made use of the sacred site. Despite their eagerness, the group had waited to start the journey home until they had made a detour to the Taos Pueblo to express their gratitude. They had to stay an extra day to enjoy the feast the Taos Pueblo held in their honor. It had been a celebration with drums and dancing, and the tourists had no idea that it was not a show for their benefit.

Much of the high country was still covered in snow, and the streams and rivers were swollen with the spring thaw. They stayed in the lowlands, actually following county and state roads much of the way now that there was no need for stealth.

The journey was finally over. Kidwell urged her appaloosa into a lope, and the others followed willingly. She forced herself to slow to a trot as they neared the house. She both longed for and dreaded what she would see when they topped the last ridge. It had been nearly a year. Even with Hank Thomas looking after the place, it was likely some thief or vandal had made their mark.

Smoke rose from the chimney and everything was neat and tidy. *What the heck? Who's at our place?* Kidwell thought. She didn't have to wonder long. Admiral O'Hare himself exited the backdoor and ran to greet them.

"So the wayward return," the Admiral said.

"To a much warmer welcome than we expected," Kidwell said.

Anna was a little more direct. She dove off her horse and nearly knocked the Admiral off his feet as she locked him in a rib-breaking hug.

The Admiral laughed. "Good to see you too, Anna."

Kidwell introduced Aisha, Greg, and Martin to Admiral O'Hare.

"John," he said when the introductions were complete. "My name's John. You can drop the Admiral crap." He looked up at Kidwell. "That means you, too. I'm retired now."

Kidwell tilted her head, contemplating the possibility. "Call you John? I'll try, but I don't know. It feels like calling the Pope by his first name."

Anna's gelding finally realized that no hand held the reins. He looked to the barn, and started walking toward his familiar stall. The reins dangling on the ground impeded his progress. The thin leather thong on the breakaway piece on one snapped, but it slowed the gelding, and he stopped after stepping on the second rein.

"Nice one, Anna," Kidwell said.

"I can fix it," Anna said, dismissing Kidwell's comment with a wave of her hand.

Kidwell's gelding neighed loudly and then shook his entire body, rattling Kidwell with a special emphasis on her kidneys.

The group laughed, adding to the celebration of the moment. "We better get these animals put away and fed," Greg said.

As though in answer to Greg's words, Sam brayed so loudly that Hank Thomas would appear a half hour later, saying he had heard his mule calling. Anna led her horse, with Aisha and her bay following. Kidwell, Greg, and Martin paused near the house long enough to unload the panniers from the mules. As they were unsaddling the animals and putting them in their pens, the Admiral's wife appeared from the house, bearing a plate of fresh-baked oatmeal cookies. Introductions were delayed while the companions descended on the treat like locusts on wheat. Even Sam got one when he reached to take it directly from Aisha's hand.

"I'm glad I got through that with all my fingers," Aisha said, her eyes wide in surprise at the mule's skill as a thief.

"It's oats. He must have assumed it was for him," Greg said.

While the animals munched on pans of oats that truly were intended for them, the humans walked to the house, as excited as the animals had been to see the barn. The group walked and laughed, every word taking on the aspect of great hilarity.

"A bath, I can't wait to take a real bath," Anna said.

"I can't wait for you to take one," Kidwell responded.

Anna laughed as she tweaked her lover's ear.

The Admiral and his wife, Lois, acted as host and hostess, even though it was Kidwell and Anna's home. The two women had been gone a long time, and the O'Hares now knew what food was where. Coffee and tea was soon made, and each of the five travelers was seated at the kitchen table with their chosen form of comfort food. Aisha held a bag of fudge-covered cookies as if she was protecting a treasure, and Greg and Anna were consuming chips and salsa as fast as they could stuff them in their mouths. Kidwell leaned over her cup of French vanilla coffee, made from freshly ground beans, and sniffed the cup as though she had caught a whiff of heaven. Martin slowly peeled an orange with an air of reverence. The Admiral and his wife stood in the background, ready to provide the returned travelers with anything they might want or need.

"Damn," John O'Hare said. "Honey, now I know how you felt all those times when I returned from a tour at sea."

His soft-spoken wife raised one eyebrow and looked at her husband. "I think not," she said, "But maybe now you have a clue."

"I hope you ladies don't mind that we took over your house while they're building ours," the Admiral said.

"Of course not," Anna answered. "Thank you for looking after it for us."

"You always said we were welcome any time," the Admiral said.

"And now you know we really mean it." Kidwell raised her face from the steaming coffee. "What's this about building a house?"

"I finally retired," the Admiral responded, "And Hank Thomas helped us find a place with a hundred acres down near the fire station."

"Hot dog!" Kidwell responded.

"So you finally decided to come home," Anna said.

"It's nearly finished. The septic, water, and electric are all in place. We already have the RV set-up and ready for us to live in until they finish the house, but we wanted to look after your place until you got home."

Kidwell blinked to hold back the tears. "Thanks, Admiral." Kidwell cleared her throat, ready to change the subject. "How are things in Washington?" Kidwell asked.

The Admiral shook his head. "Amazing. There is still an over-abundance of assholes, but Desert Lighting did something to them."

"What do you mean?" Kidwell asked.

"While they weren't overly worried about killing hundreds of thousands of innocents in the War on Terrorism, and they weren't worried about dancing right into another world war, they are terrified of looking like idiots." The Admiral ruffled his own hair. For a moment, the strain of his recent days in the capitol read clearly in the lines of his face. "There are still lots of threats and posturing, but the warmongers are afraid to order massive strikes. They just don't want to look stupid."

A knock on the backdoor ended the conversation. Hank Thomas walked into the house without waiting for a "come in." Kidwell and Anna jumped from their chairs to greet their friend and fire chief. Hank whooped with joy and picked them both up off their feet in a bear hug that popped joints and triggered moans.

"You're home!"

"Naw, we're a figment of your imagination."

Hank raised his nose and sniffed. "Well, Miss Figment, mind sharing some of that good coffee of yours?"

"Help yourself," Kidwell answered.

Bedlam followed. Conversation flew like a flock of startled pigeons. Everyone had something to ask. Everyone had something to say. Anna was totally at home, feeling as though she had stepped into a typical holiday environment of her huge Hispanic family.

Kidwell leaned close to Hank, so he could hear her over the din.

"Did my retirement check and the savings cover everything?" she asked. "Do we have any financial fires we need to extinguish?"

Hank laughed until his mustache bobbed up and down. He looked to John O'Hare. "She wants to know if there was enough money to cover everything," Hank called.

John smiled even more broadly and raised his hand for attention. "Quiet up, everyone. You all need to hear this."

It took a little time, but all the strands of conversation finally stilled, and everyone looked to the Admiral.

"You want to give them the good news or shall I?" the Admiral asked Hank.

"Go for it. You managed most of it."

"Kidwell, you and Anna gave Hank here power of attorney, and he asked me to help with some decisions. I hope we did what you wanted." The Admiral turned to Greg and Aisha. "We've been in close contact with your sister, Greg, since you and Aisha gave her power-of-attorney for your business."

"What the heck has happened?" Greg asked.

"You know the books Kidwell and Aisha have been giving to the Taos for safe-keeping?"

"Yes," Kidwell said.

"A fellow out of Oklahoma City name of Ben Tenkiller, a Cherokee man, called here, wanting to talk to someone about printing them, and I took the call," the Admiral said.

"But they aren't finished yet," Aisha said.

"He had a plan for that. He's been putting them in binders. As new chapters are available, he makes them available for sale, and people can add them to the binders." The Admiral paused, taking a sip of coffee. "Seems Ben had a dream or vision or something telling him he was supposed to give your stories to the world."

"Did he do it?" Aisha asked.

Hank and the Admiral both smiled. "Durned tootin'," Hank said. "And he's been paying Kidwell and Aisha twenty-five percent in royalties."

The Admiral walked into Kidwell's office and came back with a printed profit and loss statement. He handed it to Kidwell.

"This is the report for the last quarter," he said.

Kidwell looked at the paper, and her eyes widened as comprehension took shape.

"Oh, my God," Kidwell said. She looked at Anna, handing her lover the paper. She was deeply perplexed. "Sweetheart, should we accept this?"

Anna looked straight to the bottom line, and her eyes widened. She laughed and looked at her lover. "If we accept Spirit's responsibilities, why should we not accept the gifts?"

Kidwell sighed. "We only did what we thought we were supposed to do, but I'll admit I'm looking forward to our quiet life again."

Once again, Hank and the Admiral exchanged meaningful glances. "Kidwell, that may not be possible," Hank said.

"What do you mean?"

It was Hank's turn to make his way into Kidwell's office. He returned with two stacks of letters, each about five inches thick.

"These are just the ones from this week. We hired a woman in town to respond to the letters. For most of them, she just sends a form letter saying you're unavailable to respond at this time." Hank held out one stack of letters to Kidwell and another to Aisha.

Aisha took her stack, but Kidwell looked at hers as if he was holding a rattlesnake.

"How many letters have there been, Hank?" Kidwell asked.

"Hundreds," he answered.

"Some are more critical than others," the Admiral added. "Some of the letters demanded attention. We've been responding for you as best we can, but they need you."

Kidwell pushed back her chair and stood from the table. "I need to think about this."

Kidwell walked through the kitchen door. Anna stood, but Aisha placed a hand on Anna's arm, stopping her movement.

"Let me," Aisha said.

Aisha moved at a trot, catching up with Kidwell as she walked the trail by the house and into the woods. They walked together in silence until they came to a spot in the woods overlooking the creek below, and Kidwell stopped.

"This is one of my favorite places," Kidwell said. She walked to where a rounded root from a Ponderosa pine made a natural platform, and she took a seat at the edge of the platform overlooking the creek. "Anna and I call this the fairy throne."

Aisha sat beside her. "Fairies—after what we've both seen over the past year, I wouldn't be surprised to learn that this truly is a fairy throne."

Kidwell laughed. "You're right. I'd really like to meet a fairy."

"There's balance in the world. We know that. If there are creatures like the man who had Anna and I kidnapped, why wouldn't there be magical creatures as beautiful as fairies?" Aisha said. She paused, listening to the gurgle of the stream. "Do you think he was the only one?" she asked.

Kidwell shuddered. "Since when has nature ever created one of anything?"

They sat in silence once again. Aisha waited until she sensed it was time to speak.

"Did your guides not tell you we had more to do?" Aisha asked.

"No, wait," Kidwell said, pausing to think. "Perhaps...perhaps they did." She turned to face Aisha. "My experiences aren't like your conversations with Khadija. Sometimes it's more like they download information in my heart and mind so that I'll have it when I need it."

"And?"

"When Hank said we still had more work to do, I heard the truth."

"And?"

"And it broke my heart."

"Why?"

"Aisha, people will make it about us. No matter what we say, there will be people who think we're the answer," Kidwell said.

"Probably," Aisha responded. "But we aren't responsible for anyone except ourselves, Kidwell."

"Look what they did to Jesus' work. Look what they did to the work of the Prophet."

Aisha put an arm around her ally's shoulders. "And where would the world be if Jesus and the Prophet had not done their best, knowing as they did that there would be those who abused it?"

Kidwell leaned against Aisha, grateful that she did not carry the burden alone. This was a load not even Anna could truly understand nor share.

"We'd be up shit creek," Kidwell answered. "Aisha, why us?"

"You already have that answer. Because we asked, because we listened."

Aisha took her arm from Kidwell's shoulders. They sat in silence, listening to the call of ravens in nearby trees and the gurgle of the creek below.

The sound of insect wings buzzing near her head made Kidwell raise her hand and wave absently at the air. She paid little attention. Dragonflies were a part of the beauty of the spot. She heard a sharp intake of breath and turned to see Aisha staring just beyond Kidwell's head, wide-eyed with amazement. Kidwell followed her gaze and looked directly into the eyes of a tiny flying woman. Behind her was a small flock of similar beings.

"Well, I'll be darned," Kidwell said.

Aisha laughed. "Just when I thought nothing else could surprise me."

Kidwell smiled, wondering what other gifts awaited her in this wondrous universe. It was a universe worth fighting to save. It was worth doing her best for the universe.

The fairies disappeared as quickly as they had appeared. They didn't fly away. They simply disappeared.

"Let's go home and tell the others," Aisha said.

"Besides, we have letters to answer," Kidwell responded.

"Later," Aisha said. "Even messengers deserve a vacation now and again."

About the Author

As a writer and consultant, Kayt C. Peck has worked with many diverse organizations over the years. She found wisdom in the words and lives of people of all colors, religious beliefs, sexual orientation, nationalities, and socio-economic classes. Her multi-cultural exposure heavily influenced the writing of *Kiva and the Mosque* and flavors almost all her work. Her life-long career as a writer has included working as a journalist, a public-affairs officer in the U.S. Naval Reserve, and as a grants expert writing applications raising over $30 million for worthy domestic and even international organizations. She has published five other novels, one biography, and written many plays, including being a two-time awardee in the Rocky Mountain Voices play competition and receiving a special award for Excellence in Play Writing at the American Association of Community Theatres Region VI 2015 finals. She has authored and published numerous articles, short stories, and poems. The first edition of *Kiva and the Mosque* and her novel, *Good Water*, were both finalists in the New Mexico/Arizona Book Awards. Today, she lives quietly in her cabin home in the mountains of northeastern New Mexico.

Other books by Kayt

Good Water- ISBN- 978-1-939062-87-1

The dry plains drew Judy Proctor like a bear to her den…or a moth to the flame. Ranching was her life. The sweat as she branded or "doctored" cattle…the howl of a coyote in the quiet, night air…half-frozen fingers as she cut the wire to loosen hay bales for hungry cattle scratching for survival in snow-covered land…all of the everyday existence on the ranch was her life.
It was where she belonged.
It was a lonely life.

She had tried to leave the ranch to join the "normal" existence of a talented young woman in the city, but it had never been home. When her parents were killed in an automobile accident, she returned to the family ranch as much because she needed it as it needed her. She faced a lonely life to be shared with no better company than Somegood and Useless, her cow dog and the mottled mutt that were her companions.

Kathleen Romero slipped into Judy's life unexpectedly. She came to the plains to write a story. Would she stay because of the real truth she found in the simple drama of husbanding land and animals?

Unfortunately, even wide-open spaces can be plagued by prejudice and closed-minds. As the two women struggle to know each other, they must also carve a place for themselves among the country-folk who have been Judy's friends and neighbors her entire life.

The Ladies Room - ISBN - 978-1-943353-09-3

A dream is housed in the dusty, unused storage room above the Pink Triangle, one of Amber, Texas' two gay bars. Journalist April Sims serves as the reluctant leader in making that dream a reality. Under her guidance an eclectic group of women build a safe place in a community where being a lesbian can be dangerous and difficult.

April meets Sophia Mendez, a local attorney, as she seeks legal guidance for members of the group. In meeting with the women of the Ladies' Room, Sophia finds herself dealing with personal as well as professional issues.

When a radical religious group levels an attack on the entire gay community, even to the the point of a vigilante attack on the Pink Triangle, the strength and unity of the women of The Ladies' Room will be tested to the core.

Only time will tell if the beauty of the dream can override the ugliness of a harsh reality.

Prairie Fire - ISBN – 978-1-943353-47-7

Judy and Kathleen were accepted, even loved, by their conservative ranching neighbors. Their world felt safe and secure…until…until prairie fire! The flames disrupted their lives, causing destruction and injury, but the community pulled together to face a common enemy. When Kathleen's unofficial "daughter" found herself homeless, Pookie joined that community, bringing to this simple world her black clothes and rebellious nature. Together, conservative and liberal, gay and straight, they were a community, ready to face fire itself. The surprise to them all was the unseen enemy from within, one that had the potential to destroy them all.